The Homesteader's War

Former Union soldier and Colorado rancher Ned Bracken wants nothing more than to enjoy a quiet life with his family. Instead, he's hounded by representatives from the railroad who want him to sell his land to make way for a new track to be put down. But when raiders burn his ranch and kidnap his wife, Ned is pushed too far. Now he's out for blood and determined to find his beloved wife, Betsy. In a race against time Ned must battle outlaws, tie-down artists and ghosts from his troubled past to rescue Betsy – and also redeem himself in his own personal war.

By the same author writing as Bill Grant

Blood Feud

The Homesteader's War

Doug Bluth

A Black Horse Western

ROBERT HALE

ISBN 978-0-7198-2556-9

The Crowood Press
The Stable Block
Crowood Lane
Ramsbury
Marlborough
Wiltshire SN8 2HR

www.bhwesterns.com

Robert Hale is an imprint
of The Crowood Press

CHAPTER 1

'That's fine shooting, son,' said Ned Bracken, with a smile.

'Thanks, Pa!' his second son, Davey, shouted back.

'We'll get you learning your three R's just yet, Davey.'

'Three R's?' asked Davey.

'Ridin', Ropin' and Rifling.'

'Sure thing, Pa. I'll get an A in every one,' Davey's grin matched his father's. Ned watched him aim the Winchester for another shot at the tin cans. They were on the western edge of the Bracken homestead, in southern Colorado. Ned liked to take his boys out and practise shooting before the sun set. With the sun in their eyes it made aiming tougher but Ned thought it would hone his sons' skills.

As Davey sighted his rifle, Ned saw a small cloud of dust billowing in the distance. He heard a shout and signaled his son to stop. 'Hold up Davey, I think it's your brother.' Ned's eldest son, John, rode into view on his Appaloosa. He was fourteen, four years older than Davey, and nine years older than Sam and Emma, the twins.

'Pa! Hey, Pa!' John pulled his reins as he approached them, easing his horse to a walk.

Ned waited until his son had come to a complete stop,

5

then said, 'What's with all the ruckus, Johnny?'

'Pa! There's a group of men at the house talking to Ma!'

'What men?'

'There're four or five of 'em, one of them is dressed real fancy-like. You better come, Ma looks right agitated.'

'All right, I'll be right there. Davey, stay here with your brother.' Ned guessed what this was about. Wasting no time, he jumped onto his horse, Ole Ross, a sturdy quarter horse he had raised from a colt, and rode back to the ranch.

The Bracken homestead was about three miles from where they were shooting and Ned covered the distance in a few minutes, riding Ole Ross hard. When he got there he saw his wife, Betsy, standing on the porch, her blonde hair waving in the wind, arms crossed. A man on a black horse, wearing a fedora, leered down at her. Several other men waited around the mounted man, their horses grazing nearby. Ned reined up his stallion, dismounted, and strode up to the house, his steps measured.

'Ned!' Betsy saw him first. The horseman turned, sneering at Ned.

'Well, Bracken, I was just telling your missus here about our sweet offer. . . .'

'I know what your offer is, Gordon, and the answer is still no. My homestead ain't for sale. Now get off my property before something ugly happens.' Ned's eyes narrowed as he fingered the handle of his Colt .44 revolver, holstered on his belt.

'Now, Mr Bracken, that is hardly a way to speak to a fine, upstanding employee of the Denver and Rio Grande Railroad.' A new speaker came forward out of the group of men surrounding the ranch. His voice became rich and oily smooth; he wore a tailored suit, and brand new boots that looked as if they had never seen a stirrup. A thin mustache distinguished his face.

'Fine employee . . . Gordon? Ha! You must be his employer?'

'Indeed, I am his employer, Mr Bracken. My name is Maximilian Snodgrass, of the Denver and Rio Grande Railroad Company. You may call me Mr Snodgrass. I am here to make you a most generous offer.'

'Your fine employee, Mr Tanner, has already told me your offer, Mr Snodgrass, and I'm not selling my ranch.'

'Mr Bracken, the railroad needs to put down track to Alamosa. The shortest route is across your land. Now as Mr Tanner has told you once or twice. . . .'

'Three times, this is the fourth.'

'Now, Ned, may I call you Ned?' Snodgrass asked.

'No!' Ned's voice rose in anger.

'Well, Bracken, on behalf of the Denver and Rio Grande Railroad I am prepared to offer you five thousand dollars for your homestead.' Snodgrass's tone had an air of finality to it.

Ned looked at Snodgrass and mulled the offer over in his mind. Five thousand was a lot of money, more than twice as much as Gordon had offered when he had asked Ned to sell. But Ned's father had taken this land on a government grant, and Ned had inherited it after his passing. Besides Ned didn't like the way these railroad men did business, he still felt he was being undersold.

'I'm afraid, Mr Snodgrass, that I will have to decline your offer. The Flying W isn't for sale to you, no matter what the price. Now, if you will remove yourself and your men from my property, I'd appreciate it.'

Snodgrass shook his head slowly, 'That's real unfortunate, Mr Bracken, really too bad. This was a one-time offer. All right, boys, like the man said, let's saddle up and head back to Colorado City. Gordon, you too. Don't be giving Mr Bracken any stare-downs now.'

Ned never took his eyes from Gordon as the hired gun followed Snodgrass and the other men. Gordon turned around and gave a slight nod to Ned, his face expressionless, then after the others mounted up they rode north, toward Denver. Finally, as the riders reached the horizon, Ned let his breath out.

'Oh Ned,' Betsy ran to him. 'I was so scared. Do you suppose they're gone for good now?'

'I don't know, Betsy,' Ned hugged her tight. 'I hope so, but these railway men can be persistent.'

'That Gordon man is awful; the way he looks at me, I feel so uncomfortable.'

'He's a hired gun; I don't think he works directly for the railroad. Still, he's one to watch out for. My wish is we don't have any trouble from him.'

'I'll call the boys for dinner. Emma was just about to set the table.'

'Don't bother, I was out with Davey target shooting, I'll go get them.'

That night after dinner, Ned walked alone to water the horses. A cold wind whipped across the darkened plains. As he approached the stables a horse whickered, but Ned didn't recognize it as one of his. The rancher drew his gun. 'Who's there?'

'Hello, Ned,' Gordon said as he rode his black gelding from behind the stable.

'I thought I told you to get off my land, you no good varmint!' Ned held his gun at his side but did not holster it.

'Relax, Ned, I couldn't care less about you selling, I'm just here to give you a warning. The Denver and Rio Grande has been robbed twice in the last month. One of my jobs is to bring in the gang responsible, the Dustin brothers. I tracked them to this region and lost them. They may be still about, so keep your eyes open.'

'Thanks for the warning, but why are you helping me?'

'I told you before I don't care if you sell or not, I still get paid either way.' Gordon turned his horse and trotted away, then said over his shoulder 'Oh, one more thing, Bracken: one way or the other the railroad will get your land. Just another friendly warning.' He whistled shrilly and his horse took off at a gallop.

Ned felt a cold chill go up his spine at Gordon's last words. He didn't know what game his former comrade-in-arms was playing. He had never told Betsy but there was a reason Ned knew Gordon became a hired gun after the war; the two of them had a past. He didn't like or trust the man but knew him well enough not to take his threats lightly. He would have to be wary now.

The next several days saw calm return to the Bracken homestead. Ned and his two most trusted hands were rounding up stray cattle to get the herd ready to move to Kansas. Harry Crumpet and Lucas Deville had been with the Bracken family ever since Ned's father got a land grant from the government. The two ranch hands had fought with the elder Bracken during the Mexican War. Pa had kept in touch with his old war buddies and invited them to Colorado Territory when he got the grant, to help him. Ned thought of Harry and Lucas as uncles, part of the family, especially since his own father died while Ned was fighting the Confederates.

9

Ned's other ranch hands were only seasonal; the herd was small enough that the three of them could handle most of the duties, along with Ned's boys. It was a struggle sometimes to keep afloat. Ned had no luck as a farmer so he switched to ranching; even then it was tough. But someday the Flying W would be the talk of the West, his beef would be eaten everywhere from New York to San Francisco, that was the dream. No one would kick him off his land, railway money or not; he was here to stay.

'Hey, Ned, I think we've rounded up the last of the strays,' Harry said as he rode toward them.

'Thanks, Harry, when Lucas gets back we'll return to the main herd. . . . Say what's that black cloud, looks like smoke?'

'Ned, were the boys burning anything today?'

'Not that I'm aware of.' Ned watched as a plume of thick smoke rolled over the horizon near the ranch. His gut wrenched as realization swept over him.

'Harry, get Lucas now and meet me back at the house! Quick!' Ned dug his heels into Ole Ross and they bolted down the trail. He was a good five miles from the house but he covered the distance quickly. Ned's mind was a blank, he didn't want to even think about what he might find when he got to the ranch.

Ole Ross was sometimes ornery, and even slow. But today he must have sensed his master's urgency because he ran like the wind. Ole Ross covered the five miles to the homestead in record time. Ned pulled his Winchester from its scabbard as he approached the ranch house.

When he got there, he muffled a sob. The house was on fire; ash and smoke stung his eyes and hid Ned's tears as he leapt off Ole Ross. The homestead his recently passed Pa had built, that he had helped build, now burned, and his wife, and children . . . Ned didn't want to think of it. He was about to run into the inferno when a shout stopped him.

'Pa!' It was Davey. 'Pa!' Carrying his rifle over his shoulder, with dirt on his face, he was trying hard not to cry, but tears streamed down his face.

'Davey! What happened here?' Ned rushed to his second son and scooped him into his arms.

'Oh, Pa! The bad men came. They killed Johnny and took Ma!' Davey started crying again and anger swelled in Ned. He heard the sound of hoofs and looked up: Harry and Lucas were riding hard to the ranch house.

'Holy . . . what in the hell happened, Ned?' Harry stopped short when he saw Davey crying in Ned's arms.

'Marauders, haven't figured out who yet. You boys scout the perimeter to see if anyone is hiding out. I'll stay with Davey,' Ned's voice was pained. He tried hard to control his anger as his son sobbed quietly in his arms. They stepped away from the ranch house and Ned closed his eyes so he wouldn't watch it burn.

Soon Harry and Lucas returned carrying Emma and Sam. Both kids were crying. Lucas got off his horse, shaking.

'We found the twins near the livery. No sign of anyone else.'

Ned shook his head; he had no words as he looked at his three surviving children. It was all he could do to keep from crying, but he had to be strong for his children, to give them hope.

'We've gotta find who done this, Ned.' Lucas's voice barely registered but Ned could understand him.

'I'll get whoever did this,' he replied softly. Ned stood up, attempting to shake off the grief that had overcome him. The ranch house burned bright, smoke choking out the sun, and his children were hungry and scared.

'Harry, were there any horses left in the livery?'

'One or two have gone missing, but the rest are there, milling around outside. Someone took them out of their stalls.'

'Get 'em clear of the building. Is the ranch the only one on fire?'

Harry nodded.

'All right, but I want the horses clear of the stable just in case. Meet me down by the creek with the horses. Lucas, get the wain and load up as much tack and supplies as you can from the barn. Oh, and find rifles too. Davey, why don't you get on your Uncle Lucas's horse with your sister.'

'Where we going, Pa?' Davey asked.

'Down to the creek.'

'What about our house?'

Ned took another look at what was left of his father's labors. The fire kept burning hot and there was nothing Ned could do to stop it. He set his jaw in determination and said 'Let it burn. The important thing is that we are safe.' They rested for a time at the creek that ran through the homestead. It wasn't a very large creek, but there was enough water to keep the herd satisfied until they were moved to the railhead in Kansas. Soon Harry came with the quarter horses, riding one and leading seven others. Lucas arrived shortly after that riding in the big work wagon pulled by two draft horses.

Lucas pulled up next to Ned and whispered in his ear, 'The house is still going but it's mostly smoke now.' Ned nodded without saying a word. 'All right, Emma and Sam, I want you to get into the wagon; your Uncle Lucas is going to take you to the Nordlinger's homestead. Harry, you hold up one second while I talk to Davey.'

The youngsters hugged their dad and allowed themselves to be placed in the wagon by Harry without crying. Ned waited until the wagon was out of earshot, waving to his two youngest children as they made their way to the Bracken's neighbor, the Nordlingers. The rancher wasn't on the best of terms with Pat Nordlinger but figured he would make an exception when Lucas told him what had happened.

Ned turned to his now oldest son and said in a soft voice, 'Davey, tell me what happened.'

Davey looked at his father and took a deep breath. 'I was outside feeding the chickens when I saw men ride up to the house. They were shooting and hollering so I went to get my rifle, I left it near the chicken coop. But they were riding hard and by the time I got the Winchester they were coming straight for the house. I heard Ma screaming and some shots being fired and then I . . . I hid, in the chicken coop. I was scared, Pa!'

'That's OK, Davey, there's no shame in that. Who were these men? Did they come with the railroad men?'

Davey shook his head. 'I never saw them before, Pa. I saw them take Ma though. They had her tied up and put her on one of our horses then they lit a torch and burned the house. Johnny came out of the house then, he was bleeding real bad, he tried to aim his Colt at them but they just shot him until he was dead. They laughed and rode off with Ma. I couldn't help crying after that. I ran to help Johnny, but by then the fire was too hot.'

'Don't worry, son, Johnny is with Grandpa now. Do you know which way these varmints rode?' Davey pointed west.

'All right, now I don't want you to worry about this, I'll get Ma and bring her back. Right now, I need you to be brave for the twins. Go with your Uncle Harry to the Nordlingers and tell them what happened, tell Mr Nordlinger to tell the marshal in Trinidad what happened here. It's an important job and I'm entrusting it to you. I'll meet you at the Nordlinger ranch soon, and I'll bring Ma with me.'

Davey nodded silently and mounted one of the horses Harry was leading. The hand turned as he was riding away and asked 'What are you going to do, Ned?'

'You know what I am going to do, Harry, and don't even think about coming with me or trying to follow me. I need you and Lucas to see to my young ones because I'm coming home with their mother. I'll be back soon enough? Get me a canteen for water, and did you bring any jerky? Give me that Winchester too. Yeah, I'll need that buffalo gun, and that box of shells. Oh, and a bedroll too.'

'Ned, I can. . . .' Harry started to say as he handed Ned the supplies.

'Don't even think about it, Harry. I need you and Lucas to take care of my children and the herd until I get back. And I am coming back with Betsy, and with those bastards dead.'

With that Ned got on his horse and rode in the opposite direction to Davey and Harry. He couldn't bear to watch his son leave, in case he had second thoughts. Ned had been a cavalry scout during the war so he could track well enough. He would find these bandits and take back his sweet Betsy, and maybe even get revenge for Johnny's death. If the railway was behind it, then there would be hell to pay.

CHAPTER 2

Ned bore down over Ole Ross's neck, encouraging his trusted mount to keep a hard pace; he didn't want to lose the trail of the killers. At the same time he needed to find Gordon Tanner. The riders had left plenty of signs of their passing. Davey was right about what direction they went in. Ned counted the tracks of ten separate horses. A big gang. The railroad was clearly sending a message to him, if they were behind the raid. Gordon's last words came back to him; Ned figured they would hold Betsy as blackmail until he sold his ranch. Ten men were too many to confront head on, but he wanted to know where they were going to hold Betsy. Then he would have words with Gordon, a man who had no compunction when it came to killing.

The sun began to set and Ned's thoughts wandered to his children. Johnny, his firstborn son and named for his grandfather, was dead. Tears came unbidden down his face. During the confusion and chaos of getting his other three kids to safety Ned hadn't had time to think about John. Now, riding alone, Ned wept. He couldn't come to terms with Johnny's death now; he hadn't even seen his body. When he got back to the ranch he would sort through the ashes and give Johnny a proper burial with his whole family in attendance. But first he needed to find Betsy and bring her safely home.

Davey was right; the tracks led west toward the mountains, specifically McGovern Pass. Up there nestled in the southern Rockies was an old abandoned mining camp; the gold had been tapped out a few years before. It was impassable in the winter but now in the early spring the pass was open.

Ned followed the horse tracks until it was dark, then he picketed Ole Ross and prepared camp. He didn't make a fire for fear it would attract the kidnappers. Instead he chewed the dried jerked beef that he had brought with him. That night his dreams were haunted by John. He woke up at first light and set to tracking. All day he scouted as the ten horse trails gradually narrowed into one. Ned knew he was close to Cheyenne country, and these bandits must have known it too. They were trying to hide their numbers in case they were being tracked. Ned hoped they didn't suspect he was their tracker.

Ned continued on, warily. He checked his Colt, holstered on his belt, tapping it lightly on the butt. It had been a long time since he had had to use his revolver for anything other than target shooting. The two rifles, his Winchester and a buffalo gun, would be useful if he had range on them.

As dusk turned to darkness he finally stopped for the day, letting Ole Ross rest, graze and drink water from a nearby spring. Again Ned didn't light a fire, instead eating a can of cold beans. He tossed and turned that night and ended up lying awake, though he tried to sleep. Thoughts of Betsy and Johnny filled his head, sorrow mixed with anger. He focused his mind; only finding Betsy mattered. Finally, exhaustion took him in the wee hours before dawn and he slept.

In the morning Ned saddled his horse and started out, skipping breakfast. Speed was of the utmost importance now. By mid-morning Ned came to a creek, winding its way down to the Arkansas River. The outlaws' tracks ended here, but Ned suspected the gang had ridden in the creek for a while. It was shallow here and would be an easy way to shake any pursuers. Ned followed the brook north for several miles, hoping that he was correct, that the outlaws would hit McGovern Pass. He was leaning over Ole Ross's neck to watch the ground for horseshoe prints when he heard a loud banging noise in the distance. Ned drew his pistol and urged his mount forward at a slow pace. He found cover and went to ground in the brush.

He tied Ole Ross to a nearby tree and let him graze and rest a bit. Removing his Winchester, Ned slowly crept toward the noise. As he got closer, voices drifted through the air to his ear. Ned instinctually cocked his rifle. Peering through the leaves he saw what looked like a makeshift mining camp, with tents spread out along the creek bank. Prospectors were wading into the creek, panning for gold. He counted half a dozen men. Ned stood up, but kept the Winchester cocked and strolled into the camp.

'Hello!' he shouted, so they would hear he was coming. One of the men closest to Ned looked up, and the rancher lowered his rifle.

'What can I do fer you, stranger?' the prospector replied in a friendly manner, although Ned noticed he eyed his nearby gun belt.

'My name's Ned, Ned Bracken, I own a ranch down yonder near Trinidad. I was looking for a gang of men that might have come up this way. I was wondering if any of you might chance have seen them.'

'Name's Burt,' the prospector walked over and the two men shook hands. 'Can't say I've seen anybody come up here, just you in fact. 'Course we've only been here a week or so. Did they come this way before then?'

'No, they would have made it here yesterday most likely.'

Burt shook his head, 'I can ask the other fellers. Maybe they saw someone when they were prospecting further down the creek.' The other prospectors came over to where Burt and Ned stood after Burt hollered for them. None of them had seen the outlaws, but they claimed it might have been easy for them to sneak by the camp during the night.

'Any luck finding gold?' Ned asked.

'Maybe,' said one of the other men. 'What's it to you?'

'It's just that these men are outlaws. They're not above stealing from prospectors, I'd imagine.'

'Don't worry, Phil, he ain't after your gold, just a concerned citizen, aren't you, Bracken?' Burt asked as he slapped Phil's back.

'You could say that. No law in these parts, nothing reliable anyway. So a man has to do what he has to do.'

'Truer words never said. Well, we'll keep our eyes out for them outlaws. Thanks for the warning. Sorry we weren't much help.'

'No problem, thanks for your time.' Ned touched his hat and turned around. The men had been cordial to him so he saw no reason not to return the sentiments. Still, he never understood prospectors. Occasionally he would sell beef to a mining camp, but they would spring up and go bust so fast that it wasn't a stable source of income. The men were driven by greed. The lure of a fast dollar, which slipped through their fingers just as quickly through gambling, drinking, and womanizing, was a mystery to him. Life was hard enough on the frontier without blowing all your cash. Ned shook his head; oh well, to each his own, he thought. He made it back to Ole Ross and continued on north to the mountains.

Another few hours of riding took him up through McGovern Pass. The trail was narrow here but passable. On the other side of the pass was the old mining camp. Ned had lost the horse tracks a while back but he figured this was where they went. He got off Ole Ross to approach on foot. He climbed up a steep rise that overlooked the camp and lay flat on the ground; from there he had a clear view without being spotted. The camp looked abandoned. There were no fires, and Ned cursed out loud. To make certain no one was there he climbed down off the ridge and walked through the camp. The rancher's hunch that the camp was abandoned was right: no sign of the gang. To make matters worse, the trail went cold before the pass. Somewhere in these mountains his son's killers were loose, and they had Betsy.

He would have to pay Gordon a visit; he had no other choice. Ned didn't know if he could trust the man, but Gordon was the one who had warned Ned about these marauders, so the rancher figured he might have information about them. Gordon might have an inkling where they went or at least point Ned to someone who would. Ned and Gordon's paths since the war had taken different directions. Gordon working for the men who wanted to drive Ned off his land, something a raid and kidnapping might accomplish, stuck in his craw.

Still, kidnapping Ned's wife was low and cowardly, something even Gordon might take pause at doing. Ned wanted to make certain that the Denver and Rio Grande railroad wasn't behind it, and that it really was a wandering pack of outlaws, these Dustin brothers. To that end he would still need Gordon. If he found out Gordon or the railroad had anything to do with the raid he would never let them forget they had messed with the wrong hombre. That night he camped close to the mining camp. He picketed Ole Ross but didn't light a fire, instead just eating jerked beef. He slept fitfully again, dreaming of Betsy.

The nearest office for the Denver and Rio Grande was in Colorado City, north of the Bracken homestead. Ned figured if anyone in the railroad could help him find more information about the raid the Colorado City office could guide him to them. It took the better part of the day to get back down the pass toward the city, really just a big town. By the time he reached the territorial capital it was dark. Ned found a livery for Ole Ross and stopped at the first hotel he found, Big Pete's Emporium. It looked like a small place from the outside and would suit Ned's purposes just fine.

'I'll be needing a room for the night,' Ned told the desk clerk.

'That'll be twenty dollars.'

'You sure do love your room here, that's mighty expensive.'

The clerk coughed and blushed a little. Just at that moment a drunken dandy came down the stairs. 'Evening, ladies. If that wasn't the most enjoyable time in my life then my name is mud. I'll see you again next week.' The drunk nodded briefly to Ned as he walked out the door. Ned understood now why the rooms were so expensive.

'I'll skip the girls. I'm married. Just give me your cheapest rate.'

'Five dollars,' mumbled the clerk.

'That'll be fine. Say, you know where the office is for the Denver and Rio Grande railroad?'

'On the corner of Milton and Palmer, right next to the courthouse,' the clerk replied.

'Thank you, son.' With that Ned headed upstairs. He tried his best to ignore the perfumed ladies walking the balcony and stairs who eyed him saucily. He had loved Betsy since the first day he laid eyes on her. Ned wasn't much of a romantic man, but when it came to Betsy, he always felt she was the one. A miller's daughter, who he had wooed six years before the war. She followed him out to Colorado when his father bought the land, and she had stayed on the ranch when Ned went to fight for the Union. She was as loyal to him as he was to her and he needed her back.

The next morning Ned walked down to the railway office. A sign posted on the window next to the door read: 'Wanted for train robbery Jake Dustin of the Dustin brothers' gang. $2,500 reward. Dead or Alive.' The railroad was willing to pay twenty-five hundred dollars to see a man dead but only five thousand for Ned's ranch. Ned shook his head and went inside. The office was sparse but there was a clerk sitting at a lone desk pushed up against the back wall.

Ned cleared his throat and said, 'Excuse me, I was wondering if you could help me. I'm looking for Gordon Tanner. He works for the railroad.'

The clerk didn't bother to look up from his work. Irritated, Ned slammed his pistol on the counter. 'Excuse me, friend, but I'd like an answer to my question. I need to find Gordon Tanner. Can you tell me where he is?'

The railway worker looked up and gave an annoyed look that quickly turned to surprise when he saw Ned's Colt, its barrel ominously pointed toward him. 'No, mister, I've never heard of him. But you might want to try Mr Jenkins, he's the branch manager. He would know if we hired someone like that.'

'Where can I find him?'

'Usually he spends time in the saloon. Try him at the Hitching Post.'

Ned tipped his hat and walked out the door. As he stepped off the porch of the railroad office, a voice came to him from behind.

'So did you finally change your mind about selling to the railroad?'

Ned whipped around fast, his Colt in his hand. Leaning against the building was Gordon Tanner, his hat pulled down over his eyes. Ned holstered his gun but left his right hand on the butt and said 'Well, just the man I was looking for. You saved me the trouble of hunting you down. Now you can oblige me and tell your gang to release Betsy, and then you and I can settle up for the death of my son.'

'I have no idea what you're talking about, Ned.'

'My ranch house was burned, my son Johnny killed, and Betsy carried off by someone. And you're telling me you don't know anything about it?' Ned's eyes narrowed but his voice remained steady.

Gordon looked Ned in the eyes and slowly shook his head. 'It wasn't me or anyone with the railroad, at least as near as I can figure.' He pointed to the wanted poster. 'The Dustin brothers are causing mayhem in the area. It could be their work.'

'You're lying,' Ned said, but doubt crept into his mind.

'Nope, them Dustin brothers mean business. Jake's the oldest, the leader of the gang, his brothers are Frank and Billy, he's the youngest. There may be a cousin or two in the gang, I'm not sure. The rest are riders they picked up along the way. We go back a ways, Ned, so I wouldn't lie to you about this.'

Ned's features softened. He knew Gordon and found him during the war to be as cruel and vicious as any other varmint in the West. But this act, kidnapping another man's wife to force him off his land, was cowardly. Still, it could be that Snodgrass had made his former fellow soldier a sweeter offer than he did for the Flying W ranch. Ned wasn't sure what to believe, and since Betsy's life was on the line he had to keep Gordon close to him.

'All right, Gordon,' Ned said, his mind made up. 'I'll bite. Suppose these Dustin boys do have Betsy and your story checks out, and I won't have to kill you. But if the railroad is behind it. . . .'

'Yeah, I know, Ned; I figure you've wanted to kill me for a while now. If that's what you want, clear leather and we'll see who's the fastest. But I didn't kill your son, and I didn't take Betsy, and I didn't order anyone to do that either.'

'All right then, if you're telling the truth let's find these Dustin brothers, Gordon. I need your help either way, as reluctant as I am to admit that.'

'Well, Ned, the last information I have on them they were moving west toward the Rockies,' said Gordon.

'That's about right, since I tracked them to McGovern Pass but lost the trail. I turned around at the old abandoned mining camp.'

'We can head south and then west instead of climbing through the passes. There's a silver shipment headed to Denver from Lake City that these boys might be after.

We'll start there,' said Gordon. He flicked the brim of his hat and walked away without a word or even a glance at the homesteader. Ned bit back the words he wanted to say and begrudgingly followed Gordon down the street.

CHAPTER 3

The trip to Lake City was quiet. It took Ned and Gordon three days because it snowed on the second day out from Colorado City. The delay cost them an extra day as they waited for the sun to melt away a path for their horses. Ned tried his best to avoid Gordon, which wasn't hard since he seemed not to want to talk to Ned. So, they rode in silence. Ned still didn't trust Gordon, so he always took the first watch while Gordon slept. Then without waking Gordon for his turn at the watch Ned would fall asleep, his finger on the trigger of his Colt.

Gordon had a bemused look on his face when he woke up the first morning they were out of Colorado City. He didn't say anything but Ned figured Gordon wanted to ask him why he didn't wake him up for his watch. Ned knew Gordon to be a shrewd one and could figure it out for himself. The tension between the two was high, Ned could feel, as they finally rode into Lake City that afternoon. They found a livery for their horses, and a saloon to eat in.

'I'm going to talk to the sheriff about the shipment,' Gordon said after they ate. Ned only grunted as Gordon left and paid the saloon keeper. He thought about following Gordon but changed his mind. Instead he decided to do his own investigation into the silver shipment and the Dustin brothers' gang.

Lake City was a small mining town nestled in the southern Colorado Rockies, founded during the last silver boom that had swept over the land a few years ago. There was still silver to be mined, but not enough for the number of people who came to the town. Then news came out of Cripple Creek that gold was discovered and many prospectors left to try their fortunes there. Even with competition from other mining towns there were enough folks in Lake City to make it a lively town. As Ned wandered up the street he saw a barber shop; curious to see if he could glean any gossip he went inside.

'Need a haircut, mister?' the barber, a middle-aged man, asked.

'Nope, just give me a quick shave.'

'Sure thing, partner, looks like you need one. Say, are you new in town? Haven't seen you before.'

'Yeah, me and my . . . er associate rode in today,' Ned said, uncomfortable with calling Gordon his friend.

'Are you bounty hunters? Sorry to ask, but my last two customers were bounty hunters who just rode into town,' said the barber, leaning over as he dabbed shaving cream on Ned's face.

'I was interested to know if you've heard anything about the Dustin brothers' gang.'

'Ah, so you are bounty hunters. I don't know too much about them. Rumor has it they've been robbing trains and stages up and down the Front Range. But no one's ever said they've come to Lake City.'

'I'm curious because I heard a silver shipment is headed here. I was wondering if that was something the gang was likely to attack.'

The barber bobbed his head up and down as he finished Ned's shave. 'Yup, there's a shipment coming in by mule train from the camps up in the mountain. It comes in once a month, and the silver gets taken by stage to the railhead and then to Denver. Hey, how do you know about the silver shipment? You wouldn't happen to be one of the Dustin brothers now, would you?'

Ned stood up, rubbing his jaw to check the barber's work. 'Nah, I'm not an outlaw. In fact, I'm looking for them; they um . . . took something of mine and I want it back. Thanks for the shave, how much do I owe you?'

'Fifty cents, sir. I'm giving you a discount on account of you being a new customer.'

'I'm obliged, mister. . . ?'

'Carruthers,' said the barber.

'I'm Ned Bracken, Mister Carruthers. Let me ask you one more question if you don't mind. Who's the sheriff of this town?'

'That would be Bob Jenkins; he's the one to talk to about the Dustin gang and the silver shipment.'

'All right, thank you kindly for the information.' Ned doffed his hat to the man and walked outside. To his surprise he saw Gordon waiting outside, leaning on a post.

'Have a nice shave?' he asked.

Ned narrowed his eyes, 'Sure did, even found out who the sheriff is in this town.'

'Good, so did I, let's go talk to him.'

The sheriff was a short balding man who was working a big wad of tobacco in his mouth when Ned and Gordon walked into his office.

'What can I do for you fellers?' he asked. His feet were resting casually on his desk.

'You Bob Jenkins?' Gordon asked.

'The one and only, who's asking?'

Gordon put a piece of paper down on the desk. 'I'm Gordon Tanner with the Denver and Rio Grande railroad. This is my associate Ned Bracken. We had word that a gang of varmints is headed for your town and we want to make sure the silver shipment is protected.'

'What varmints are these?'

'Jake Dustin and his brothers: wanted in four territories for train robbery and murder.'

The sheriff put his boots on the floor and sat up straighter in his chair.

'Dustin brothers, you say? Well, I assure you that our silver is well protected even from those bandits. We haven't seen hide or hair of them in Lake City.'

'Just to be on the safe side, do you mind if we take a look at the silver?'

Jenkins scowled and shrugged. 'Sure, I suppose that wouldn't be a problem. It came down from the mining camp this morning; my deputies are guarding it now.'

The sheriff led the two of them down some side streets and almost to the edge of town. Lake City was a boom town so folks came and went as they pleased; there were several people on the streets as they walked past. When the silver veins dried up in a few years Lake City would become just another mining ghost town. He brought them to a small warehouse near the outskirts of town. It was non-descript and looked like it was used to store mining supplies. Jenkins rapped three times on the door and waited.

'This here's the place,' he said just as the door swung open. Ned heard the cock of a Winchester as they stepped across the threshold.

'Easy boys, it's me.'

'Sorry, sheriff, didn't know you were coming,' a young gunslinger said as he walked out of the shadows, his Winchester cocked and ready, sitting easily in the crook of his arm. Another man came close behind him, his hand casually waving over his holstered revolver. Each of them wore a deputy's star on their lapel. They looked twenty years younger than the sheriff.

'Boys, these here fellers work for the railroad. They want to check the silver shipment. This is Mr. . . .'

'Tanner, and my associate Mr Bracken.'

'These are my deputies, Ernest Johnson and Buddy Slade.' The two men nodded at Ned and Gordon.

'They seem a tad young, don't they, sheriff?'

The Winchester-holding deputy, Buddy, quick drew his Colt with his left hand; his partner followed suit with a gun in both hands.

Jenkins chuckled, 'My boys are quick as lightning. That's why they're deputies.'

Gordon nodded in agreement and even Ned was impressed. Both deputies were wet behind the ears but would have had him in a draw. Although Ned didn't know if either of them had been in a gunfight before. It takes more than a fast hand to survive against cold-blooded killers.

'Fair enough, but there're only three of you to guard the whole shipment. There are seven or eight members of the Dustin brothers' gang. You sure you don't need any help?'

The sheriff turned and looked Gordon straight in the eyes. 'Now look here, mister railroad man. I have a sworn duty to protect this shipment of silver. I'll be damned in hell before I turn it over to any supposed railway man. My boys will be fine. If you are so concerned you can join them when the silver leaves in the morning. They'll escort it by wagon down to the railhead and meet up with some US Marshals. It's unusual for railway men to escort shipments; are you really that concerned about the Dustin brothers?'

'Yes, we are concerned about them. Mostly because the railway has insured the silver shipment, so we want to make sure it arrives safely. Thank you for your offer of riding down to the railhead. We'll meet here tomorrow morning.'

'We leave at dawn,' Buddy said as Ned and Gordon departed, leaving the sheriff with his two deputies.

Once outside, Gordon cocked his head at Ned and smiled, 'You sure were quiet in there.'

'I figured I'd let you do the talking since I don't give a damn about the silver. All I want is Betsy back.'

'That is precisely why I'm glad you let me do the talking. If the sheriff figured you were out for blood, there's no way we would be allowed anywhere near the shipment.'

Ned walked in silence for a moment more and finally said, 'Are you sure these outlaws will take the shipment?'

'I've been tracking the Dustin brothers, all three of them, for a while. They've robbed four of our trains and at least three stages. If they are anything, these boys and their friends are greedy. They found out about the silver because they forced one of our conductors to tell them where the railroad was getting its silver cargo. It's only a matter of time before they hit this Lake City shipment. Then you can find Betsy and have revenge for your boy.'

'Maybe you and I will settle some things too, Gordon.' Ned gave Tanner a cold hard stare.

Gordon matched him, 'We can do that too. Let it go,

30

Ned, the war was a long time ago.'

'Not long enough.'

Gordon was the first to drop his gaze; he turned and walked away, calling over his shoulder, 'See you in the morning, Mr Bracken.'

Dawn came, not soon enough for Ned. He had Ross saddled and paid his hotel bill. When he arrived at the warehouse he saw Gordon already there, chatting with the sheriff and deputies. The wagon looked loaded and was hitched to a team of horses. An old man sat on the seat holding the reins in his hand. He looked absently into the gloom and occasionally spat his tobacco juice on the ground.

'This here is Gary, our driver. Ernest will take shotgun, and Buddy will cover the rear on horseback. You fellas ready to go? You should hit the railhead by the afternoon.' The sheriff stepped back from the wagon and without another word Gary cracked the reins and the team lurched forward. Ernest barely had time to jump on as the wagon peeled away from the warehouse. The sheriff waved his hat in the air and Ned and Gordon followed the wagon as it rode out of town.

Lake City was high in the mountains; the nearest railhead was one hundred and sixty miles to the northwest in Canon City. From there the silver would be shipped by rail to Denver. The road was passable, just wide enough for the wagon or two abreast on horseback. What made Ned nervous were all the easy places along the road for an ambush.

'So why didn't the marshals escort the shipment if they are so afraid of these Dustin brothers?' Ernest was talking to Gordon.

'The marshals have a lot to do and there are so few. We were mostly playing out a hunch they might show up. After four robberies my company started asking the marshals to escort the silver. We also placed reinforced steel doors in the coaches that carry the silver. It will be easier to rob the overland shipment than the train.'

They rode along in silence for a time. The only sound besides the wagon wheels and the horses was Gary occasionally spitting his tobacco juice. It had been three hours since they left Lake City and they had not seen another living soul. Ned tried hard not to think about Betsy or his dead son. His grief had turned to anger, his hope to rage. His only focus was finding the Dustin brothers. If they were truly behind the raid on his ranch and the murder of his son, he would kill them one by one. If they weren't, then he would kill Gordon.

Ole Ross's nostrils flared suddenly with a shift in the breeze. Ned focused back on the road, searching the rocks above. His years as a scout for the Union Army had honed his senses even as his tracking skills fell into disuse. Bits of scree rolling down the hill, a bird taking flight, chirping wildly, the flash of sunlight on metal glinting from a boulder and there it was.

'Ambush!' Ned's voice was lost in the crack of a rifle. Before he could breathe again Gary, clutching his chest, slumped over his seat and the team was bolting. Ernest was leaning over Gary's body trying to reach the reins while firing wildly over his shoulder. Buddy urged his horse forward, unholstering his revolver, while Gordon hit the ground with a Winchester in his hand, finding safety behind a boulder.

It had been so long since Ned had fired a shot in anger he almost froze. Then a volley of shots rang out and Ned wheeled Ole Ross into some tall grass near the road. He took his Winchester out, cocked and readied it, and found cover behind Gordon's boulder.

'Well, Ned, looks like we found them.'

'Gary's dead, and now the wagon is out of control.'

'Yeah, I don't know if the young deputies will survive. It was foolish for Buddy to chase after it. Good place for an ambush though.'

'I saw it a second too late. Dang, I'm getting old.'

'Just rusty, I imagine. Too focused on the road to notice them,' said Gordon.

'Let's see if they've got us covered. I'll use the old hat trick.' Ned took his hat off and using a stick, he poked it up over the large boulder. Two shots came whizzing by and Ned pulled his arm back.

'At least two of them are covering us with Winchesters, and they've got the high ground,' said Ned.

'Let's double back. It will take us longer to reach the wagon but we have a better chance of living.'

Ned nodded and without another word bolted straight ahead, keeping the boulder to his back, while whistling for Ole Ross. More shots fired, but Ole Ross crossed Ned's path. At a dead run Ned grabbed the reins and leaped on, putting more distance between him and the shooters. Gordon met up with him and the two rode what seemed like a mile and then took a wide turn to head north of the road.

'Now we should be parallel. We'll follow this path a few more miles and then connect back to the road. Hopefully we will be ahead of them as they try to unload the silver,' said Gordon.

Ned pushed Ole Ross hard over the rough terrain, with Gordon at his side. He felt like they were back in the war tracking Confederates side by side before things went sour between them. Time dragged on interminably, Ned never letting Gordon out of his line of sight, just in case; finally they connected to the road again.

'We must be ahead of them, let's backtrack. You got that Winchester ready?'

Ned cocked it, 'Yeah.'

They rode on and eventually found several horses grazing alongside the road. They looked familiar to Ned. Soon after they found the wagon, abandoned, Gary's and Ernest's bodies slumped on the bench, the silver gone. A little further on and they found Buddy's body, riddled with bullets, lying on the ground.

'Land sakes, these boys are good,' said Gordon as he beat his leg with his hat in frustration.

'Now what?' Ned said evenly as he tried to keep his emotions under control.

Gordon gave a deep sigh, 'They've got to sell the silver somewhere. The ore doesn't do them any good unless it's smelted. Some place discreet that will take unrefined silver.'

'And where's that?'

'Easiest place to sell is Mexico.'

'Looks like I'm going to Mexico then,' Ned said softly as he looked off in the distance with hard, cold eyes.

CHAPTER 4

Ned rode his new horse with reckless abandon. The rancher had left Ole Ross boarded at a stable until he returned. He was a good horse but Ned wasn't sure he could make it down to Mexico, and speed was of necessity now. He had spent far too long in Canon City for his liking. Gordon had to report the ambush to the railroad and the US Marshals' Office. The bodies of Gary and the two deputies had to be delivered to the local mortician, and both of them were subject to a grilling by the marshals. Ned told them about the raid on his ranch. He was ordered home by the marshals, and the railroad hired the Pinkertons to track down the outlaws.

The rancher wouldn't abide that. He sent a message to Lucas by stage that he was all right and to pick up Ole Ross when he could, bought a new horse, and discreetly left town. He didn't want to wait for Gordon, nor did he really trust him anymore. The US Marshal who talked to Ned confirmed that the Dustin gang had been roaming around southeastern Colorado. Somehow they knew when and where the silver shipment would be, and Gordon seemed to have done his damnedest to prevent Ned from stopping them. All the way to Canon City Ned hadn't said one word to Gordon.

Once their business was complete Ned tipped his hat and bid adios to his old army comrade, pretending to go back to his ranch. Instead Ned bought a horse and more ammo from the general store. If Gordon turned up in Mexico on the wrong side Ned wouldn't hesitate to gun him down. His focus was Betsy and revenge.

Ned was south of his own ranch now, nearing Trinidad and New Mexico Territory. He was avoiding the main trail to Santa Fe, instead trekking through the woods in case the Pinkertons, Gordon or the Dustin brothers found him. He slowed his horse down as he picked his way through the underbrush. Dusk was falling and Ned decided to camp for the night. He figured he was half a day's ride to New Mexico and another three days' ride to Mexico itself.

He wanted to push on but prudence won out over his desires. His horse needed rest, and Ned needed food. As he walked the horse through a particularly wooded area looking for a stream Ned felt oddly as if he was not alone.

He finally found a small creek to water his horse. Ned built a campfire and let the horse graze and drink, but he couldn't shake the uneasiness that someone else was in these woods. Within moments his suspicions were confirmed when he heard the snapping of dry twigs coming from the trees. He grabbed his Winchester and cocked it, holding his breath.

'I've got you covered you varmint, come on out.' Ned was startled when a deer, a buck, jumped out of the woods and dashed through his camp. Ned chuckled to himself; his nerves must be getting to him. He took deep breaths to keep calm, but he couldn't help wondering what had caused the deer to run through the forest like that. Curious, Ned strode away from his camp, keeping his rifle close to his body. Soon he saw more deer running and other woodland critters following the lone buck. Then he smelled it: smoke in the air. He rushed back to untie his pony and saddled up, kicking dirt on his own fire.

Instead of heading away from the fire Ned urged his mount toward it, wondering what the cause was. He found out soon enough. Near the edge of the woods was a wide clearing; in the middle teepees burned, and dead bodies lay strewn on the ground. Ned got a close enough look to determine no one was alive. A raid; someone had taken it to the Indians: Comanche, Cheyenne, Kiowa. Ned wasn't sure who the victims or the raiders were. It reminded him of what had happened during the war, some members of his own unit, Gordon too, killing innocent women and children. He shuddered at the thought.

Ned rode back to his camp, sleeping without restarting the fire. Whoever had raided the tribal camp might be indiscriminate and choose him as their next target. At least his instincts were right, he wasn't alone. Ned awoke before dawn, saddled his horse and rode on. By midday his path had crossed the main road; he passed it and kept to his underbrush trail, still wary of the Pinkertons. After a few more hours a sign at the side of the trail said 'Welcome to Deadfall, New Mexico'. The town was unfamiliar to Ned, but he figured it was worth a look in case anyone in the town had seen the Dustin gang.

The town of Deadfall lived up to its name. It was quiet as death as Ned rode down the sole boulevard. There were roughly ten buildings on either side, and halfway down the street he saw a hitching post in front of what looked like a saloon. He hitched his horse and walked through the batwing doors. The saloon was empty except for the bartender. As Ned approached, the man gave a scowl.

'What do you want?' he growled.

'Just a glass of whiskey, and some information.'

'Both will cost you,' said the bartender.

Ned threw two double eagles onto the bar. 'Have you seen a group of men ride through here? There would be seven or eight of them, possibly with a woman, headed south.'

The bartender shook his head, 'Nope, can't say that I've seen them fellas. We don't get too many folk here in Deadfall though.'

'Where is everybody? The town seems deserted.'

'Everyone's on a posse, one of our scouts said some Comanche were camped nearby.'

'What do they aim to do?'

'Kill 'em. Colonel Roberts don't take kindly to Comanche.'

Ned paused, his hand holding the whiskey glass, his face going pale at a distant memory. Without thinking he said, 'That name sounds familiar. He wouldn't by chance be Black Jack Roberts from the war, the murderer who burned family farms?'

The barkeep's eyes narrowed slightly, his mouth turning into a scowl, but he said nothing. He was young, younger than Ned, and looked like he could handle himself with a weapon. He didn't have the overconfidence of youth, but had the steely gaze of someone who has stared down death. Ned looked around the saloon for the first time, paying attention to the details: an old Confederate flag nailed to the wall above the bar, another banner, a military standard, hanging above the batwing

38

doors. During the war Ned and his company of Colorado volunteers fought against Sibley's Brigade. There was one unit in the Brigade that always struck fear in the Union soldiers: the Texas 107th Cavalry Militia, Lieutenant Colonel 'Black' Jack Robert's Raiders.

Ned watched the man closely while slowly backing away. 'Thank you kindly for the information, I think I'll be going now.' Ned kept his hand close to his Colt ready to draw if the man made a move. It was all clear to him now. After Sibley's Brigade tasted defeat, Roberts and his raiders disappeared. Rumors abounded that they hadn't gone back to Texas, but had stayed in New Mexico. Ned knew now that the rumors were true. Roberts and his gang were still here, carving out a fiefdom.

Ned was at the door when he heard horses galloping. He risked a look out the door to see maybe two dozen men on horseback riding hard for the town. The barkeep took advantage of his distraction and reached under the bar, bringing up a shotgun.

'You wait there, mister, Colonel Roberts going to want to talk to you,' he shouted.

Ned drew and fired once wild, knocking the Confederate flag off the wall. He dived under the doors just as the shotgun opened fire. The rancher ran to his horse, unhitching it and jumping on its back in one motion. He dug his spurs into the horse's flanks and wheeled it around in the opposite direction to the oncoming horsemen. Ned heard the shotgun blast again and instinctively ducked his head. The rancher put spurs to horseflesh, trying to put as much distance as he could between him and the town of Deadfall and Black Jack's Raiders.

Twilight had descended and with no sounds of pursuit

Ned eased his horse into a walk. He cursed his bad luck; there was no sign of the outlaws. Gordon Tanner and the Pinkertons were out there tracking them and possibly him, and now he had to worry about old Confederate enemies on his trail. Finally when he felt that he was safe he made camp. He barely slept, keeping one hand on his Colt and the other on his Winchester.

Jake Dustin eyed his blonde captive as she bent over the cooking fire. She was comely for having birthed three children. Her son had put up a fight when they came for her but Jake had gunned him down. She too had struggled before Jake's youngest brother, Billy, knocked her out before her husband, the rancher, returned. Now Jake was admiring her supple curves in the fading light. She had been traveling with them for four days now and had tried to escape twice. Betsy, she called herself, straightened and felt his eyes on her. 'Must you always watch me, Mr Dustin, even when I am cooking your supper?'

'Given your history of running away I thought it might be a wise thing to do.'

'Soon my husband will find you and kill you, and I won't have to run away anymore,' she flashed a cold smile. Jake thought she was going mad from grief but her eyes shone not with madness but with cold calculation. Jake couldn't suppress a shiver down his spine. He took pride in his cold-bloodedness; he had killed his first man when he was fourteen and was now wanted from Topeka to Tucson. But Jake felt uneasy in the presence of this fiery woman.

'We'll see. I am in no hurry to meet your husband, or the law. But if I do meet up with him, I assure you he will die by my hand. Quickly, if he's lucky.' Jake turned away from her and walked toward the edge of their encampment. His brothers Billy and Frank were there next to the horses, reorganizing the saddle-bags.

'You should let me have her for the night, Jake,' Billy said.

Jake shook his head. 'No, she's destined for a hacienda in Mexico. Some rich Mexicano will pay for her. I don't need her anymore used-up than she already is.'

'So that's where we're headed?'

Billy wasn't always up to speed on the plans. 'Yup, we gotta unload this here silver and cool our heels from the law.'

'That was a brilliant plan robbing the silver shipment like that,' said Frank. 'Our informant was right about the location of the wagon. Too bad we had to leave it behind. How are the horses?'

'They're weighted down with the extra loads. It will make slow going and Mexico is still pretty far.'

'Don't worry, Frank; Santa Fe is close. We'll stop there and trade out the horses. We can get a wagon to disguise ourselves a little before we cross into Mexico. Once there it will be easy living, brothers, with the senoritas.'

'How much you figure we got?' asked Billy.

'All together with the four train robberies, two stages and the silver shipment, after the cut, it might be close to fifty thousand dollars.'

'That'll be enough,' Frank said, grinning widely.

'We'll make a payout once we get into Mexico, and see who in the gang will stay with us and who won't. We can lie low or cause more mayhem, we'll have options.'

'I love having options.'

'So do I,' said Jake, with a sly smile.

41

CHAPTER 5

Ned finally reached Santa Fe the next day. His horse was about done; Ned had pushed him pretty hard. He got a room and started to explore the town. He didn't think the Dustin gang would come into the town but it didn't hurt to look. Santa Fe was much larger than Lake City and had a definite Spanish flavor. During the war Ned didn't get a chance to see Santa Fe but he and the other Colorado volunteers had fought and died to keep it in the union.

He stopped at the first gambling hall he found, getting a drink and sitting down at a faro table. The dealer was a squat middle-aged man with a weathered face. After a few hands played in silence Ned threw down a double eagle and said, 'Are you from around here?'

'Not originally, no, I came from Kansas; Abilene actually,' said the dealer.

'Must be a lot of gunslingers from there,' replied Ned.

'You're telling me. That's why I left.'

'You ever hear of a bunch called the Dustin brothers?'

'Oh yeah, the Dustin gang, they're notorious, they came from Missouri originally. They caused some mayhem in Abilene then I think they went westward toward Colorado.'

'They might come to New Mexico Territory, Santa Fe even.'

'I hadn't heard that, you might want to mention it to the sheriff. He'd be keen to chase those bandits out of town if they ever show up in Santa Fe,' said the dealer.

'I don't think it's necessary to involve the sheriff,' said Ned, thinking about what had happened in Lake City.

'In that case Al Simmons is the man to talk to. He's from Kansas too. In fact he used to ride with the Dustin gang, according to him at least. You can find him at Madame Bolivar's most nights.'

'I'm much obliged for the information,' said Ned. He doffed his hat and made sure to leave his yet-to-be-bet double eagle on the table.

The lead the dealer gave him was the first break he had gotten since he left Lake City. Ned tried to temper his hopes and focus on finding this Al Simmons. Madame Bolivar's was a bordello situated just out from the center of town. It was a two-story building across the street from the livery where he had stabled his horse.

Ned wanted nothing more than to storm into the place and force Simmons to tell him where the Dustin gang was going. But as Ned watched the entrance to Madame Bolivar's he saw well-dressed and even perfumed gentlemen enter the establishment. Ned looked at his clothes, dusty and encrusted with dirt from the long ride. He hadn't bathed in a week. If Ned was going to get any information from here he would have to dress the part, or at least make an attempt. Checking his wallet Ned counted out fifty dollars. His new horse had cost him twenty-five, and he still needed to pay the boarding fee for Ole Ross when he got back. Still, if he needed to spend money to find Betsy, so be it. He'd play the part to find this Al

Simmons. Two hours later as the sun set Ned walked into Madame Bolivar's wearing a new shirt and jacket, his face shaved. He looked like just another dandy availing himself of some female companionship for the evening.

The inside of Madame Bolivar's was posh. High chandeliers hung from the ceilings, the carpet was lush and thick, there was a bar against the far wall, and a faro table stood in one corner. Ned went to the bar first and ordered a whiskey. He surveyed the room while sipping from his drink. Scantily clad women walked their beaus for the hour up a short flight of stairs to the second floor.

A buxom brunette sidled up to him at the bar, giving him a coy smile. Ned ignored her and focused on the card game. There a lone man sat gambling, a loaded revolver on the table next to him. Ned brushed off the brunette who was trying to get his attention and walked over to the table. He played a few hands while eyeing the other man.

A tall thin man, clean-shaven, he was the only man not interested in utilizing the main services of the brothel; Ned figured he was a regular. He played in silence, sipping on his whiskey, never looking at Ned or even the dealer. After a while, and with Ned down to his last few double eagles, the thin man stood up.

'Thanks Sam, I'll see you tomorrow.'

'Sure thing, Al,' the dealer replied.

Ned raised his eyebrow slightly at the name but otherwise kept his focus on his cards, not looking at Al until he was out the door. Ned folded his cards and stood up.

'Care to spend some time with one of the ladies?' Sam, the dealer asked as Ned walked toward the door. Not bothering to answer Ned made for the street and the man he was certain was Al Simmons. As he walked out, he spotted the thin man across the street, quickly ducking inside the livery.

Ned tried to look as inconspicuous as he could, but his urge to confront this man before he got on a horse and rode off overcame him. He strode boldly toward the former outlaw. Al could lead him to the gang but Ned's horse wasn't even saddled so once he left the livery Ned would never be able to catch him.

As Ned reached the livery a loud 'He-Ya!' came from inside. He dived for cover just as the double doors swung out, kicked open by a hulking stallion, Al Simmons riding it. He took one look at Ned, sneered and pointed his gun. 'Teach you to follow me,' he said.

Ned's instincts took over; without thinking he drew and before Al could finish his sentence Ned fired. The shot hit Al in the right shoulder, making him shoot wild. Howling in pain, he dug his spurs in, causing his horse to rear. Al lost his grip and landed on the ground. Ned stood over him, his gun pointed at his face. He kept his hand steady and his voice calm when he said, 'Are you Al Simmons?'

Al said nothing, only grinding his teeth, his eyes filled with hate.

Ned pulled back the hammer of his Colt. 'Al Simmons of the Dustin brothers' gang?'

'I don't ride with them no more. I ain't responsible for anything they done.'

'So you are Al . . . Good, tell me where your gang is.'

'I told you I don't ride with them, I don't know where they are,' said Al.

'When did you leave them?' Ned asked.

'At the Colorado-Kansas border we robbed two stages, and I was ready to cash out. Jake, he's the leader, told me he had something big planned, but I wanted out.'

'When was this?'

'About three weeks ago. I been down here in Santa Fe ever since. Please, mister, I need to see the doctor, I feel woozy.' A soft moan escaped from his mouth.

'Almost done, Al. How many men does Jake have and where in Mexico will they be heading?'

'He's got two brothers and maybe six or seven other guys. I don't know if he recruited someone else when I left. I wasn't the first to leave.'

'Mexico?' Ned said sternly. 'Then I'll give you some water.'

'Jake said he has a deal with a Mexican landowner. He didn't name him, though. I'm telling the truth, I swear.'

Ned considered what Al had told him for a moment, then handed him his canteen. The man slurped the water down before Ned snatched it back. By now several passers-by were standing around watching the spectacle. 'Get a doctor, quick,' Ned yelled. 'This man's been shot.' One man ran down the street yelling 'Gunfight.'

Ned started to walk away, then stopped and said over his shoulder, 'Just one more thing. Do they know you're here? Will they come find you?'

'They know I came south, that's it.'

'All right, take care of that shoulder now. If I catch you trying to bushwhack me, I'll take out more than your shoulder.'

Ned slipped around the back of the livery before he had to answer uncomfortable questions from the sheriff. If Al was telling the truth than he still was no closer to finding the Dustin brothers' gang. He had to find Betsy before the gang made it to Mexico. Once there, he'd never be able to track them. He walked purposefully toward his hotel, using as many side streets as possible.

When he got near the Santa Fe Grand, where he was staying, he slowed. Some instinct coming from his days when he was with the First Colorado Volunteers kicked it. It had saved his life on more than one occasion during the war, and now it was telling him not to walk into the hotel.

There were two saddled, riderless horses hitched just outside the hotel entrance. The saddles bristled with guns, two rifles tied to the saddle of each horse. This was what made Ned suspicious; it was a lot of firepower, assuming the men the horses belonged to were also carrying revolvers. Ned edged behind a barrel as two men, wearing identical hats with stars on their lapels, exited the building; the Pinkertons had already made it to Santa Fe.

One of the men checked the saddle-bags on the horses while the other looked around. Ned, as casually as he could, turned around and walked back into the deepening shadows of the night.

If the Pinkertons got to the Dustin gang first, there'd be a shoot-out and Betsy might die. Ned needed to find a new horse fast. The one he had bought in Canon City was well spent. Without stopping to think Ned walked into the first saloon he saw and asked the bartender for a whiskey. 'You know where a fella can buy a horse around here? I need one in a hurry,' he said.

The bartender scratched his bald head. 'Well, now that's a good question. I reckon if a feller needs a horse right quick, and he doesn't want to make no fuss about it, like having the sheriff around,' the bartender raised an eyebrow at Ned, 'then his best bet would be the half-breed, Juarez. He can be found near the San Miguel mission. Likes to sell horses, that one does.'

'Thanks, I'll find him,' Ned paid for his drink without touching it, and headed out.

Juarez operated out of a rundown section of Santa Fe. He had a small corral with an assortment of horses available for sale. Ned arrived after he'd stopped at the hotel to pick up his pack and rifle. He had no intentions of staying in town after he had bought a horse.

'Can I help you Senor?' Juarez asked as he sidled up to Ned.

'I need a horse in a hurry.'

'I have this fine sorrel for fifty dollars.'

'Cheaper.'

'Well, I see you're a man that drives a hard bargain so I've got two horses here each for twenty dollars.'

Ned watched as Juarez trotted out a frisky Palomino and an older claybank. Glancing over his choices, Ned came to a decision. 'Is that Palomino fast?'

'Oh, he can run. Give him his head and he'll fly like the wind.'

Ned rolled his eyes. 'That's fine, I'll take him. You have tack?'

'I have a used saddle and bridle I can part with for five dollars.'

'Fair price, I'll take it. I don't suppose anyone asks you where you acquire these horses and supplies, do they?'

'They can ask. . . .' Juarez gave a sly smile. Ned thought it was better not to ask where the goods came from. Instead he changed the subject.

'By chance have you ever heard of the Dustin brothers?'

Juarez laughed, 'Si, senor, I know them. In fact, I just sold Mr Dustin and one of his brothers two horses and a pack mule.'

Ned couldn't contain his excitement. 'When?'

48

'Last night.'

'Do you know which way they went?'

Juarez shrugged, 'Don't know, but I think one of them mentioned Mexico.'

'Thanks.' Ned saddled up and kicked the Palomino into a canter, heading south. He could catch up to them now; the pack mule would slow them down.

CHAPTER 6

Jake stared over the plain. The Comanche raiding party was getting smaller as they faded into the distance. Satisfied they were gone, Jake stood up from his squat and walked back from the ridge. The way would be clear tonight and tomorrow; the Comanche never raided the same place two days in a row. Three more days of travel and they would be in Mexico. He was getting tired of riding, and his gang was starting to complain. Then there was the captive. The sooner he was rid of the home-steader's wife the better. He had been tempted more than once to slit her throat while she slept or just abandon her in the wild. But the thought of losing all that money restrained his hand. The *ranchero* would pay one thousand dollars for her. That was sweet money, and more than enough reason to put up with her attitude. Betsy would lash out at Jake or his brothers every chance she got. But she was truly scared of Dead Eye Conner.

Dead Eye joined them when they reached Santa Fe. Jake had ridden with him in Kansas, but he was never a member of the gang. Dead Eye came and went as he pleased. Jake had heard the outlaw went south, but hadn't realized he was in Santa Fe. When he and Billy went to pick up some fresh horses from Juarez, Dead Eye was there. He half-suspected Juarez had tipped him off.

Jake didn't know his real name, but Dead Eye suited him; a phony eye-patch over his left eye, he was a dead shot. Faster than Jake or any of his *desperadoes*. He also didn't say much, which made his reputation that much fiercer. His look could chill someone to the bone. That's what he did to Betsy. Jake had to smile to himself; if anyone could tame the wench it was Dead Eye, he thought, walking back to the men.

'Looks like the Comanche aren't headed toward us, and it doesn't look like there is another raiding party in sight. We'll head on down to the valley and make camp there. Two or three more days and we'll be in Mexico, boys.'

A faint cheer went up from the seven assembled men.

'Where's Dead Eye?' Jake asked.

'He's watching Betsy draw water from the creek,' said Billy.

Jake nodded, 'When they get back we'll go. Word from Juarez is that Pinkertons are in Santa Fe, so we have to make tracks to get some space between us and them.'

'There must be a reason that Dead Eye joined up with us after all this time,' mumbled Frank.

'Maybe there is, Frank, or maybe I just like your charming personality.' It was Dead Eye, walking Betsy back with skins full of water. He fixed Frank an icy glare as he walked by. Frank shivered.

'We ready, Jake? I heard you say the Comanche are gone.'

'Yeah, they're gone, let's saddle up and get out of here.'

Without another word the ten of them got on their horses and took the short, steep trail down to the valley below, Dead Eye in the lead. Jake trailed behind, leading the pack mule loaded with the stolen silver.

Ned kicked the ash from the old campfire. He bent down and held some of it between his fingers, then let the wind blow it away. It was still warm, couldn't have missed them by more than a few hours. He walked to the edge of the mesa. The trail down was pretty clear, the outlaws not trying to hide their passing. He scanned the horizon; the mesa was elevated high above a flat plain, but Ned couldn't see any horses. They were moving fast, but Ned was on the right track now; the rancher knew he'd catch them before the border. Ned jumped on the Palomino stallion and carefully picked his way down the mesa.

Ned heard the sounds of battle before he saw it. War whoops and gunfire filled the air. Ned slowed his horse and unpacked his Winchester, readying himself. His heart beat faster, palms sweaty; the Dustin gang must be close. Then the acrid smell of smoke hit his nostrils. The Palomino whickered softly and Ned had to lean down to calm him. Something was burning. Ned dug his spurs in and the stallion reared. He took off at a gallop just as dawn's first light cracked the horizon. Ned had risen early to try to make up ground on the outlaws.

As he broke through some underbrush, he saw a pillar of black smoke rising in the air. Flames leaped from a burning structure, a homestead. As Ned drew closer, he saw a Comanche raiding party, with twenty to thirty braves surrounding the building. Another shout came from the east. Ned pulled up the Palomino, and saw another group of riders bearing down hard on the Comanche. Ned rode his horse behind some tall sagebrush. He was about a half-mile away from the burning homestead, close enough for an eagle-eyed brave to spy him. The raiding party's attention had turned to the group coming at them. The rancher felt a cold chill run down his spine as he could finally make out the new riders. One of them held aloft an old regimental Confederate flag. It was Roberts's Raiders. Ned could see Roberts now, the wild-eyed and now fully bearded face of the man who had given the Second Colorado Volunteers such fits during the war.

Jack Roberts was a man unto himself. Even after the South's surrender he was still fighting the war, vigilante style. Ned was unsure of what to do. He had no love for the Comanche, whose raids just as easily might hit Ned's ranch back in Colorado, but he knew Roberts was dangerous. The two groups of raiders met and Ned made up his mind. He could slip around the battle and continue heading south to find the Dustin brothers and Betsy.

As he moved around the fight, trying to remain inconspicuous, he saw the same bartender from Deadfall. Too late, their eyes locked, and even though Ned was still a good two hundred yards away the man recognized him. Ned saw him point straight at him and shout something to Roberts, who stood tall in his saddle, two guns blazing, as he mowed down any Comanche in his sight. The colonel nodded to the bartender and shouted an order. Three men broke away from the battle and rode hard after Ned. Still holding the Winchester Ned wheeled his horse around. Roberts's three raiders were five hundred feet away when Ned opened fire. Three bullets, crack, crack, crack, and three horses were riderless.

The nervousness that Ned had felt earlier when confronting the lone bartender in Deadfall or even Al Simmons in Santa Fe, was gone. This was different. Ned knew battle and his instincts came back to him. The

Comanche, seeing three of Roberts's men down, pressed their attack. Ned holstered the Winchester in its scabbard, and just glimpsed Roberts, his face contorted in fury as he watched Ned gallop away.

Jake dug his spurs into horseflesh, pushing his mount faster. The pack mule was slowing them down; he almost regretted getting it. But the raw silver was too heavy to carry on the horses. Dead Eye Conner kept the pace fast, almost as if he wanted to leave Jake behind. That concerned Jake greatly; if Dead Eye wanted to take over his outlaw band, Jake wasn't sure he could best him in a fight. Not for the first time Jake wished he hadn't agreed to let Dead Eye join them.

'Slow up a bit, Conner,' he yelled. 'This danged mule is making me fall behind.'

'Well hurry up, Jake, we've got to get to the border 'afore those Pinkertons catch us.'

'Well, that's what I'm saying, the pack mule carrying all the silver and the money we robbed from them stages is too slow. You got to slow your pace. We'll get to Mexico soon enough.'

Dead Eye wheeled his horse around and confronted Jake. The whole gang was watching them now. 'Listen here, Jake Dustin, if you want me in this party then we follow what I say,' he said angrily.

'Oh no, Dead Eye, you've got it wrong. You see this here is my outfit. My brothers and I started it and the men here are loyal to me.' Jake tried to keep his voice from quivering as Dead Eye's hand inched toward his holstered gun.

'Are you sure about that?'

Jake said nothing, but glanced at his brothers. Both cocked Winchesters and aimed at Dead Eye. A little more reluctantly, the others reached for their guns. Dead Eye was fast and would surely kill Jake and one or two others. But he couldn't get them all before he was gunned down. After a long moment Dead Eye rested both his hands on the pommel of his saddle. Jake shuddered slightly in relief.

'All right, Jake, here's what we do. Since you owe me and you can't keep up with my pace, I'm taking the girl and I'll meet you in Mexico. If you don't catch up I'm selling her to our mutual friend. If the price doesn't cover your debt, then I'm coming back for you. You get me?'

Jake said nothing, his palms sweaty, only nodding his consent. With one hard look that made the other two Dustin brothers back their horses up, Dead Eye rode over to Betsy.

'Come on, darling, you're coming with me. Say tootle-loo to your friend Jake now.' Betsy's face betrayed genuine fear when Dead Eye led her away. Jake had never seen her eyes that wide in terror in the entire time she had been with him. He cursed softly to himself. How he wished he had never run into Dead Eye; now he had to explain himself to his gang.

As Conner and the rancher's wife rode away without a backward glance, Billy and Frank both gave him accusatory looks.

'Now what was all that about owing him?' Frank asked as Billy nodded vigorously. The rest of the gang were all looking at Jake.

'It's a long story, but Dead Eye and I did a few jobs together before you and Billy teamed up with me. You could say he got me out of a few jams and perhaps I took more of the money that we stole. He thinks I owe him and with Dead Eye it's better not to argue over a debt. I didn't intend to bring him along. I didn't know that he was in Santa Fe when that danged horse trader Juarez must have told him we bought horses from him.'

'This ain't good, Jake, not at all. Some of us are counting on that money. Maybe we were better off with him leading the group,' Frank spoke up. Some of the others nodded and mumbled to themselves.

'I know where he's going, don't worry. I'll handle Dead Eye and get the money for the girl. All of it.'

The middle Dustin brother remained unconvinced. 'If you say so, but I've heard of this Dead Eye, rumor has it he's killed dang near twenty men in shootouts. Are you saying you're a faster shot?'

'No, I'm saying I'll take care of it, Frank. We'll bushwhack him either before or after he ransoms the girl. In the meantime we've got to catch up to him and keep ahead of the Pinkertons.' With that Jake spurred his horse and pulled on the pack mule's lead. He didn't look back to check if the others were following.

Gordon frowned at the Pinkerton detective standing in front of him. 'Are you sure they passed through here?'

'The half-breed is a good source of information. We aren't far behind the Dustins. We'll catch them.'

'Can the sheriff spare any men?'

The detective scoffed, 'We'll have more than enough men when we meet up with the other unit of detectives. Your bosses at the railway really want these outlaws found. They're paying a pretty penny.'

'Yeah, we'll find them. Juarez tell you anything else?'

'Just one more thing: another man asked about the Dustins too. He bought a horse from Juarez and took off in a hurry when Juarez said he had seen Jake Dustin last night.'

Gordon nodded, unsurprised. 'Was he a tall feller, kind of dusty blonde hair and wearing a wide-brimmed hat?'

The Pinkerton shrugged, 'Juarez didn't say, just that he seemed rushed. Someone you know?'

Gordon shook his head slightly, 'No one we can't handle.'

'All right then, we'll leave in one hour. Your only job now is to advise. Once we find the gang my men and I will handle things, you stay out of it. I don't want any liability claims for a dead railroad employee. Are we clear?'

Gordon wanted to deck the smug little detective. He was young with a thin mustache, and Gordon doubted he had ever been in a real gunfight. The president of the railroad had insisted the Pinkertons get involved despite Gordon's objections so he, ever so slightly, doffed his hat to the man.

Taking it for a yes the Pinkerton said, 'All right, Mr Gordon, get your horse ready, I'll attend to my men.'

The detective was good but not that good. He hadn't followed up on Al Simmons's shooting in the livery. The former outlaw hadn't talked to the sheriff about who had shot him. But Tanner, on his way to the sheriff's to find out any information he had on the Dustins, had overheard him talking to the doc about who the shooter was. Now Gordon knew that Ned was out there chasing after Betsy and revenge.

CHAPTER 7

Ned wanted to put some distance between himself and Roberts's Raiders. He knew he had just made a powerful enemy and wanted to keep as far away as possible. All day he rode the stallion hard until he could go on no further. He rested for the night, letting the horse drink his fill of water. Ned figured they had come pretty far from Santa Fe. Within a day he should catch up to the Dustin brothers, the pack mule slowing them down. That night he spent cleaning his Winchester and his Colt, making sure both were fully loaded before he slept.

The next morning he readied his gear and saddled the Palomino. He promised the stallion he would go slower today, and Ned meant to keep that promise. The last thing he needed was for his horse to wear down and strand him in the desert. As he rode he saw signs of the outlaws. The pack mule's tracks were distinctive, so Ned figured he could follow them until he found Betsy. Once he had caught up to the gang Ned didn't really have a plan.

He thought about rushing in with guns blazing and mowing them all down. The fight with Roberts's Raiders had gotten his blood going and in his heart this was what he wanted to do. But that didn't seem realistic. Instead, he needed the high ground, some mesa or ridge overlooking the party. Then he could pick them off one by one.

The ground was becoming rockier and in the distance Ned could see some mountains along the horizon. Now all he needed was the Dustin brothers taking the low road through the valleys of the upcoming mountains. It would be faster for them to do so. If they were rushing to make it to Mexico then there was no reason for them to take the high ground.

As he reached the edge of the mountain range Ned saw the tracks of the pack mule and over a half-dozen horses riding straight into a narrow valley. Ned urged the Palomino up a winding trail as he approached the first mesa that led to the larger mountains. He wanted to get ahead of them now so he could set up before they came.

Gordon had to admit he was impressed with the Pinkertons. The four detectives who rode with him met up with five others, led by a Kiowa scout, at a predetermined destination south of Santa Fe. They were all heavily armed. The nine moved in concert following the Kiowa, an expert tracker who found signs of the gang. They were good, the reason the railroad had hired them. He still had not told them about Ned Bracken. Gordon didn't think Ned would be too much of a problem. As long as he didn't get in the way.

Gordon rode up to the lead detective, Thomas Masterson, and tried to strike up a conversation. 'How good is this Kiowa scout?' he asked.

Thomas, looking annoyed, said, 'He's one of the best, has never failed us.'

'What's his name?'

Thomas shrugged, 'He rarely speaks. I'm not sure he

even understands English. He communicates by sign language, mostly.'

Gordon nodded and remained silent, thinking the conversation over.

'When we find them you stay clear. We'll handle the Dustins.'

'I heard you the first time you said it in Santa Fe,' Gordon replied, giving the Pinkerton a look of disdain.

Thomas stopped his horse short and Gordon had to wheel his horse around to face him. 'Listen, Mr Tanner, I'm serious. I know you were in the war and you are in charge of security for the Denver and Rio Grande railway. But we are professionals. I don't need to be held liable for a dead railroad worker. Now, now don't get mad, Gordon. You're tough, but believe me when I tell you the Pinkerton detectives will take care of the Dustin brothers' gang. There are plenty of parties that will pay to see those three brothers swing.'

'As long as I get a share and my boss gets what he wants.'

'I'm sure he will.' Thomas flicked the reins and moved ahead, trying to keep the Kiowa tracker in his sights as he moved further ahead of the group.

Gordon wanted to speak to the Kiowa scout. Yesterday they had come across a burned down homestead and the signs of a Comanche raid and battle. He had thought they should stop and search for signs of the Dustin brothers, but the Pinkertons had overruled him. 'No need to tarry here. It looks like the family escaped, but not before they took some Comanche down,' he had said.

Gordon wasn't convinced, but he kept his mouth shut. Thomas promised to investigate further once they had caught the Dustins. One glimpse of the scorched land as they rode away caused Gordon's stomach to churn. He saw a shred of a Confederate battle flag caught on a sage brush. Gordon had heard rumors about some old members of Sibley's Brigade that did not go home to Texas when the war ended. If Roberts and his Raiders really were ravaging New Mexico, killing Comanche, and otherwise dispensing vigilante justice, then they could have run into the Dustin brothers and taken their stolen silver. That was a situation that Gordon didn't want to dwell on too much. The Pinkertons would be no match for the Raiders. On the other hand, Roberts might have killed Bracken. That would be one less worry for Gordon.

Jake was still nursing his bruised ego when Billy led the party into the canyon. He was wary of an ambush; the ridges were tall with large boulders strewn around that could easily conceal a man, or group of men.

'Billy, are we going the right way?'

'This way is faster I think, Jake.'

'If you say so,' Jake muttered to himself. He should have taken the lead instead of allowing Billy to. But he didn't want to be too far from the loot. He trusted his brothers well enough but the other men, after the show-down with Dead Eye, might mark him as weak, and either turn tail or steal the silver.

Jake scanned the canyon walls for an ambush, his right hand resting near his rifle, while he steered his horse with the left. His brother, Billy, suddenly stopped his horse and turned around to say something. At that moment the crack of a rifle sounded and Clint, who had kept riding past Billy, cried out and fell out of his saddle.

'I've been hit,' he screamed as he clutched his chest. Red rivers of blood poured out as he gasped for breath.

Billy turned his horse completely around and headed straight for Jake. The rest of the gang tried to follow him as another rifle report filled the air.

'Get down,' Jake yelled. 'Find cover.' He cursed himself for letting his guard down. He knew better than to ride blind into a canyon. It was how his gang always preferred to set up their ambushes.

'Do you see him?' Frank asked.

'He's on the ridge to the right, I think,' said Billy.

'Just one?'

'We have to assume there's more than one,' said Jake, from behind a boulder. 'A posse may be up there waiting to string us up.'

'Clint's gone,' Billy wailed.

'Yeah, he's a goner,' Jake tried to keep his tone calm. Clint Braddock was a good man, had been with the brothers since the beginning, but he knew the risks when joining the gang. They all did.

Another shot sounded, and the bullet kicked up dust in front of Jake. The horses and mule started to run the opposite way, away from the shooting. Jake tried to see the shooter, but the ridge was a good two hundred feet high and the shooter had the sun to his back.

Jake, in sudden inspiration, took out a handkerchief. It was red, not white, but it would have to do. Spying a small stick on the ground near him, he grabbed it and tied the kerchief to it. Poking his head just above the rock he held the handmade surrender flag high and waved it back and forth.

'We surrender. If you want the silver it's on the pack mule. Just let us go and it's yours,' he shouted, to perplexed looks from his brothers who had managed to crawl their way closer to Jake.

There was a pause in the shooting and then a voice shouted back at them. 'What about the woman? Let her go unharmed, and when she's safe, we'll talk about your surrender.'

Ha, thought Jake, the rancher. Now, to find out if he was alone. 'We've got her, she's holed up not far from here. Come on down and we'll take you to her.'

'Not on your life, Dustin. I'd sooner kill the lot of ya, right here and now, and find her on my own. Now hand her over or taste more lead.'

'You try that, you danged fool, and my man will kill your pretty wife,' Jake yelled back.

There was no sound from the ridge, and Jake knew he had him. 'Let us get through the canyon then we'll let her go.'

'Not a chance, I don't trust you.'

'Well then, looks like we're in a standoff, eh rancher?'

'Looks like it, but I've already got one of you, and I'm a crack shot with this rifle. One by one I'll take out the rest of your gang.'

Frank had crawled his way over to Jake, struggling to get his breath. 'What in the hell are you doing, Jake?' he said in a harsh whisper.

'I'm trying to buy some time. That darned sidewinder has the high ground and can pick us off like he said. If we get him to talkin' then he might get distracted and one of us will,' he looked meaningfully at his brother, 'corral the horses and get us the heck out of here.'

Frank nodded slowly as realization hit him. 'So am I going alone or is someone coming with me?'

'I don't care how you do it, just get those horses. We'll escape while one of the gang provides some cover fire.'

'All right, I'll get them. You can count on me.'

'I know I can, brother,' Jake said with a smile. His brothers were not the smartest apples in the family tree but they were so very loyal to him, and loyalty mattered to an outlaw like Jake Dustin. He could guide and teach them and hope that they would learn, but at the very least they would follow him to the ends of the earth.

A close shot shook Jake from his thoughts. 'I hear you whispering down there. No tricks, I want my Betsy delivered to me unharmed,' said the rancher.

'We've got to send word to our man to let her go, otherwise he won't know. You won't let us go to her, you won't let us take you to her, how about we tell you where she is and you can go get her?'

'No way, Dustin. You'll just send me on some wild goose chase and then escape again. I've tracked you too long and far to let you go without Betsy.'

'Well then, how do you propose we resolve this here standoff, rancher?'

There was a long pause and then, 'Well, you made a big mistake by separating Betsy from your gang, if that is in fact what you did. For your sake I hope you didn't kill her,' there was a slight catch in the rancher's voice. Jake didn't want this homesteader to rampage through him and his men if he thought Betsy was dead. Truthfully Jake had no way of knowing if she was or wasn't but he needed to reassure the rancher.

'No, a pretty young thing like her is worth way more alive than dead. There are many men who would pay handsomely for a blue-eyed blonde lady like her.'

Two shots fired in rapid succession. 'That's enough talk about Betsy from you. As for resolving our current impasse, I'll give you this proposal. It looks like you are

64

telling the truth about my wife not being with you, so I will allow you to send one, and I repeat one, of your men to find her and bring her here. Someone loyal to you that won't run off, like a brother. Pick one of them to bring Betsy to me. In the meantime you'll be my hostage.'

Jake didn't like the sound of this. This rancher was more cunning than he thought. He had already sent his brother to get the horses, and he was still hoping that he and his gang might escape once Frank got back. As he was thinking what to do, he heard a voice speak up, 'I'll go get her, Jake. I volunteer.' It was Billy.

'Who said that?' asked Bracken.

'Billy, Billy Dustin, youngest brother to Jake and Frank.'

'Why that's right brotherly of you, Billy Dustin. You have a horse?'

'They ran back north out of the canyon when you started shooting.'

'How far away is Betsy?'

'Not far,' Jake replied. 'Billy could walk there,' He couldn't help but feel pride at his little brother's courage.

'That's good news for Billy. Come back by sundown with my wife or your brothers die. You better start walking.'

'You ain't gonna shoot?' Billy asked.

'Nope,' came the one-word reply.

Billy scrambled to his feet with one look at Jake, who only nodded in reply. He started walking south straight out of the canyon, the way they were headed. Jake hoped to pick him up once Frank brought the horses back.

As Billy walked out of sight, the rancher cocked his rifle. 'I have plenty of ammo so you better hope your little brother makes it back before sundown.'

Jake hoped his brothers would come through for him and not leave him with a gang of questionable loyalty at the hands of a vengeful rancher.

CHAPTER 8

Ned wiped the sweat from his brow. He pulled his hand back and watched it shake slightly. As he watched the younger Dustin outlaw walk quickly away from the pinned-down gang Ned wondered if he was doing the smart thing. It wasn't really smart to ambush a party of ten men by yourself, especially when you were low on ammo. He checked his saddle-bag. Only four rifle cartridges left and probably seven or eight men. Ned hadn't planned this ambush out thoroughly; once he spied the outlaw band riding through the canyon, he reacted quickly. He selected an ambush site and started firing as soon as they came into range. The rancher didn't think through the consequences, only anger and rage took hold of him. Ned wanted to kill them all for killing his boy and for taking Betsy.

Luckily Betsy wasn't with them otherwise they could have used her as a hostage. But now Ned had to wait and hope that Jake was telling the truth. Once he had Betsy safe he could deal with the gang. If Billy didn't come back with Betsy alive then he would be true to his word and kill Jake Dustin. His hand had stopped shaking now as he took some deep breaths. He really needed a partner to help him; the problem was he trusted nobody. Not with Betsy's life.

Ned took a long pull from his canteen. Keeping one eye on the outlaws hiding on the canyon floor, he reloaded his rifle. So far none of the gang had moved except for one who had inched toward Jake. Their voices carried to Ned but they were too garbled for him to make out what they were saying. The whispering had stopped after Ned fired a shot and the Dustin gang had been quiet as church mice ever since. Ned took them for cowards but was reluctant to underestimate them. If they were planning some way of escape, he didn't want to be caught off guard.

The sun was starting to hit the horizon now and still no sign of Billy. Ned wasn't too surprised although he had held out some slight hope that Betsy would appear. If they killed her. . . . No, there was no need to think about that. But Jake Dustin was about to pay at the very least for killing Ned's son.

'Time's almost up, Jake. Where's your brother?' Ned steadied himself against the rocks, taking aim with his rifle at the last location he saw Jake. Ned spied a boot heel sticking straight out in the fading light. He cocked the Winchester and said, 'Come on, Jake, I know you're still down there. If Billy isn't here by the time I count to ten, then I'm going to start shooting, and I ain't gonna stop until you're all dead. Of course if one of your men was to volunteer you for summary execution then I might be willing to let him go free.'

There was no reply, so Ned checked the wind one more time and began counting down. He figured he had enough sunlight to shoot by the end of his countdown. By the time he got to five he heard a loud shout. At first he thought it was Billy returning with Betsy and his heart leaped in joy. He looked to the north but saw nothing. Instead, another louder whooping came, followed by the thundering of hoofs. Ned nearly cursed out loud as he saw the gang's horses galloping full bore from the opposite end of the canyon. A lone man on horseback was driving them while pulling a pack mule. Ned aimed his rifle quickly, intending to take out the rider, when a shot from behind blasted the rock next to him.

'I seem to have forgotten your pretty wife, rancher, but I remembered some lead just for you.' It was Billy's voice. He had doubled back and ambushed Ned just as the horses were being driven toward the remaining outlaws. Trapped, Ned dropped the rifle and spun around with his Colt in his hand, firing toward Billy's shot. There was a loud thud and then, 'That was close, Bracken, but you missed.'

Next it was Ned's turn to dive to the ground as Billy returned fire, two shots in rapid succession. A holler from the canyon floor, 'Come on, Billy, put an end to that rancher and let's get to Mexico.' Jake and the rest of the gang had mounted their horses and were heading further south out of Ned's line of sight. Billy fired three more bullets and Ned stayed on the ground, looking for cover behind another boulder.

'So long, rancher, don't be following us now. Your pretty wife will be in some hacienda soon. Take it up with the rich Mexicano who buys her.' Ned heard the retreating footsteps of the youngest Dustin brother and almost cried out in frustration. He was so close but had let them slip through his grasp. Ned thought he must be losing his edge to allow a young scallywag like Billy Dustin to sneak up behind him and bushwhack him. Now the whole gang had disappeared again and Ned's hopes of finding Betsy alive were fading.

Jake couldn't believe his luck. His brothers had come through for him. He hadn't even planned it this way, hoping to pick up Billy on the way out of the canyon. But the foolhardy kid had taken some initiative and done something right: providing enough distraction for Jake and the rest to get on their horses and ride out of rifle range. He hoped that Billy had killed the rancher or at least wounded him to the point it kept him off their trail.

As the group reached the end of the canyon Jake looked behind him, but couldn't see much in the fading light. Then, a sound. Sure enough it came again, a shout. He held up his horse and got his revolver ready. A shadow moved toward him; Jake raised his gun and shouted, 'Stay where you are!'

'Jake, it's me, Billy. I done took care of that rancher.'

'Billy, all right you made it. That was quick thinking taking out our tail.'

'Heh, thanks Jake, I doubled back after I reached the end of the canyon and found a trail leading up the back way to the top of the mesa. I sneaked up behind him and waited real quiet. I almost bushwhacked him when Frank shouted. That's when I opened fire on him.'

'Did you kill him?' asked Frank, who had ridden over when he saw Jake stop.

'Well, I don't know. I laid down a lot of lead. He ain't following us any time soon, that's for sure.'

'All right, Billy, saddle up and let's get going. We still got a long way to Mexico.'

Gordon waited patiently next to Thomas, the nameless

Kiowa scout busy looking over the tracks and the remains of the battlefield. They watched him in silence. Two of the Pinkertons were hovering over the lone body left on the canyon floor while two more were digging a nearby grave. Other detectives milled around, and a few were on the bluff scouting.

'Quite a battle our little outlaw gang ran into?' Thomas spoke first.

'Looks like an ambush,' Gordon replied.

'Yes, well possibly, let's see what our Kiowa friend has to say.' The head detective motioned for the scout to come over to where the two sat on their horses. 'What say you, Kiowa? Did our friends survive this ambush? If so where did they go?'

The scout only nodded his head and pointed to the opposite end of the canyon.

'Excellent. Once my men finish burying that bandit we'll be on our way. Gentlemen,' Thomas left Gordon, riding his horse closer to the shallow grave, giving his men directions. Once he was out of earshot Gordon leaned over and said to the Kiowa, 'Scout, how many men ambushed the Dustins?'

The Kiowa looked at Gordon quizzically then raised one finger. 'Just one, eh?' Ned Bracken, Gordon thought.

'Do you speak English?'

The Kiowa only shrugged.

'What's your name?'

At first the scout looked away and Gordon figured he didn't understand the question. But he was looking toward Thomas. Seeing the Pinkerton fully engrossed in his task of ordering his men around the Kiowa turned his head back to Gordon and said, 'I will not give you my Kiowa name, but you can call me Great Tree.'

71

'So you do know English,' Gordon said, pleased.

'I speak to only those whom I wish to speak to.'

'I suppose that doesn't include the Pinkertons.'

Great Tree shook his head. 'I work for them, they pay me dollars. I do not want them to know anything about me.'

'But you take their money, you have no problem with that,' said Gordon.

'I take their money, yes this is true. I take it because I know there will be a time when my people, despite some who still wish to fight, will finally surrender. We cannot win against the Cavalry or the settlers, so I acknowledge this fact and take their money. When the time comes I will be ready to care for my family. I do not think my people will be treated gently but I will have done enough for my own kin to keep them alive. They will not starve as long as they have the white man's money.' With that Great Tree turned and walked, back bent, following the tracks that led out of the canyon.

Gordon marveled for a moment at the cunning the man displayed. Thomas seemed the pompous type, so it was unsurprising for him to easily underestimate a savage Indian. But Great Tree had worked for other Pinkerton detectives and to fool them all into thinking he could speak no or very limited English took skill. The Indian had one skill that was useful to the detective agency, and he didn't need to speak to do his job. Whatever the case, Gordon wanted to ask him about Ned or Colonel Roberts's Raiders but now reconsidered it. The Pinkertons took the Kiowa to be a mute, or at least with a minimal understanding of English, and were blissfully ignorant of Ned's existence. He wanted to keep them that way. Gordon would deal with Ned on his own terms.

He trusted the Kiowa to say nothing to the Pinkertons, and he didn't want Great Tree to know that he had knowledge of Ned. Gordon flicked the reins and trotted his gelding toward the Pinkerton as his men were shoveling the last of the dirt onto the dead man.

'Shall we be off?' asked Thomas.

'Whenever you're ready; the scout picked up a new trail, and time is money.'

'Indeed it is, your employer's money,' said the detective. With that the rest of the detectives loaded up their horses and got ready to ride out of the canyon.

'Two more days and we'll catch them.'

'You know that for a fact?' asked Gordon.

'Just a detective's hunch, my friend.' Thomas spurred his horse forward, not waiting for his men to be ready. Gordon eyed the top of the mesa and saw the two Pinkertons up there jump on their horses. They were quick responders these Pinkertons were, and didn't waste time, which was good news for Snodgrass and the railroad. Gordon had little doubt they would catch the Dustin brothers. And that's what really worried him, he thought, as he flicked the reins and followed the Pinkertons away from the ambush site.

Ned waited for the Pinkertons to ride by, then crept out slowly from the cave he had found, pulling the reins of the Palomino. When Ned found the hideout at the edge of the canyon, he first thought that Betsy was there, but it turned out to be empty. He rested there until dawn wondering what to do, when he heard the soft tinkling of bells. Crouching low behind a rock with the Palomino standing behind him, he cocked his Colt and steeled himself.

A Kiowa stood in the mouth of the cave, his shadow a

silhouette against the rising sun. Before Ned could breath he disappeared like a ghost. He waited for a time then heard the telltale sign of thundering hoofs followed by shouts. Ned caught a glimpse of one rider's hat; only the Pinkertons wore derbies like that. He figured the Kiowa was a scout hired by the detective agency. What he didn't know was why the Indian hadn't told the Pinkertons he was in the cave. He didn't want to dwell on the notion so he put it out of his mind.

But now he had a way to track the Dustins; just follow the Pinkertons. Ned had to get to Jake before the detectives did otherwise he might never find Betsy. Saddling the Palomino quickly he found the Pinkerton tracks and rode at a steady pace, not too fast but enough to keep close.

CHAPTER 9

Betsy Bracken looked askance at the gruff man riding beside her. He hadn't said more than two words to her since he first joined the outlaws and subsequently took her for himself. She only knew him as Dead Eye, which is what Jake had called him. He had a big scar running along his neck, as if he had survived the hangman's noose. Her eyes scanned the horizon trying to avoid watching the grizzled outlaw. The gunslinger, for his part, kept studiously ignoring Betsy.

As the sun dipped Betsy noticed that it was now setting on the opposite side of the mountains. Fearing they had turned around Betsy wanted to ask Dead Eye where they were. She was still a little afraid of him and didn't want him to rise to anger against her, so she feigned ignorance. 'Are we in Mexico yet, Mr Dead Eye? I've never been to Mexico 'afore.'

She waited the span of two heartbeats, fearing that Dead Eye had not heard her. He was slightly ahead of her now, but didn't turn around. She was about to speak again when his low gravelly voice suddenly came to her ears. 'We ain't going to Mexico, woman.'

Curiosity overcame Betsy, and she replied, 'But Mr

Dead Eye, I thought. . . .'

'I know what you thought, woman, but it ain't true. And my name ain't Dead Eye, it's just what people call me.'

'But Jake Dustin said he was gonna sell me to some Mexican for money.'

'That was Jake's plan, but I'm changing it. See, I don't think I could get more than a thousand dollars for your pretty hide in Mexico. And that silver that good ole Jake is hauling must be worth twenty times that at least. Besides, I'm probably more wanted in Old Mexico than in America. I don't need no aggravation from the Mexican authorities. If Jake thinks I'm headed for Mexico than I ain't gonna discourage his thinking in that regard.'

Betsy was quiet, not knowing what to say, then, 'So you've been to Mexico, what's it like?'

'I wasn't on no sightseeing tour. I fought for that boy emperor they had. Fought for him and against him. So I made enemies all around. No thanks on returning to Mexico. That's why I made my play for you when I did. Get me a little leverage on ole Jake. If there's anything that boy loves, it's money. His greed will keep him wanting to come after you. That's when I'll git him.'

'Why?' Betsy asked.

'That darned fool owes me money. He's going to pay me or I'll kill him.'

'Have you killed a lot of men?' A cold shiver went down Betsy's spine.

'Lady, you don't know much about gunfighters and their reputations, do you?'

'Why, I'm just a modest rancher's wife, I spend my time sewing, mending and cooking. I don't pay much attention to those manly pursuits.'

Dead Eye just snorted in disbelief. 'I done killed twelve

men in straight duels, another twenty who tried to bush-whack me. I lost count of how many I killed in the wars.'

'My husband was in the war. He doesn't talk about it much.'

'No, I don't reckon he does,' said Dead Eye, suddenly reticent to talk much.

'He's hunting the Dustin brothers to find me. I know it. He'll find me, and when he does he's going to kill you,' Betsy said, steeling her courage in a moment of defiance with this cold-blooded killer.

Dead Eye reined his horse up and looked Betsy straight on, making eye contact. His words were slow and mea-sured but it was the extreme confidence with which he said them that chilled her to the bone. 'No, I don't reckon he'll do that.'

He wheeled his gray mare around and said 'Come on, rancher's wife, we've got to meet up with the Dustins, and you're my bait.'

Ned followed the Pinkertons' tracks for a day and a half. He was getting close to the border. The tracks stopped near a small town. He needed to resupply, he was almost out of bullets, and had to shoot a jackrabbit for dinner the night before. Ned headed into the town, and, hitching his horse to a post, walked into the saloon.

'What'll you have?' the portly barkeep asked.

'Water, and whiskey,' replied Ned. 'In separate glasses.'

Ned drank the water fast – his canteen had run empty – then sipped the whiskey.

'Where you from, stranger?' It wasn't the barkeep.

Ned turned around and saw a pretty blonde woman eyeing him coyly.

'You look like you've been riding a long and dusty trail,'

she said, her lips opening up into an inviting smile.

Ned tugged on his unkempt beard, 'Yeah, I've come from Colorado. Headed for the border.'

'Well, you made it, stranger, last stop is Old Mexico. What brings you down here?'

Ned didn't like her probing questions, nor the way she looked at him; he wanted her to have as little information as possible.

'Family.'

She waited, and when Ned didn't elaborate she just nodded. 'Well, my name's Sara, let me know if there's anything I could do for you?'

Ned tipped his hat, and said 'Thank you kindly, ma'am, if I need you I'll find you.' Sara waited for a moment, expecting more, but when Ned turned back to his drink, she turned and walked out in a huff, pushing hard against the batwing doors.

'Local hurly-gurly girl looking for customers,' the barkeep said after she left.

'I figured as much. I'm not interested, I already have a wife. What's the name of this here town?'

'Bittercanyon.'

'Anybody come through here recently?'

'You mean like a group of Pinkerton detectives?' the barkeep eyed Ned suspiciously. 'Yeah, they came in, resupplied at the general store and rode back out.'

'Toward Mexico?'

'No, the way they came in.'

Ned nodded thoughtfully. He wondered if the Pinkertons were doubling back, setting a trap for the Dustin gang, or if they were going into Mexico another way.

'I guess I'll resupply myself. Where can I find the

general, and the blacksmith? My horse threw a shoe.'

Ned was given the directions. He rented a room in a local hotel so he could take a bath, bought some more ammunition, and got his horse re-shod. He was almost out of money now, and hoped to find Betsy soon, otherwise he might be forced to turn back if his supplies ran low again. Ned cleaned his Winchester, and his Colt .44s, preparing them for the Dustins.

If they had already crossed over to Mexico, it would be difficult to find them. He didn't speak Spanish and didn't have much money. He hoped that the gang was still in New Mexico; in the morning he would set out to find their tracks again.

That night the sound of gunshots woke him up. He heard loud voices coming from the street. He peered out the window from his second-story room and saw a bunch of riders milling about in the street. They were well armed, and Ned counted at least twenty of them. He didn't think they were the Dustins, or the Pinkertons, but he knew they were trouble.

Then he saw, as one of the riders dismounted near a street lamp, a faded Confederate emblem on his sleeve. Roberts's Raiders were here. If they spotted him, they'd kill him for sure.

'Jeb, Matt, get us some rooms at the hotel. Kick out anyone who's staying there,' said a large man astride a big black horse. Two of the men were walking toward the hotel, and some made their way to the saloon. They weren't just passing through. Ned had to get out of here before they recognized him.

He got dressed, grabbed his gear, and loaded and belted on his .44s. He slung the rifle over his right shoulder and walked calmly down the stairs. The two raiders were talking to the hotel clerk, their backs turned toward Ned. The clerk looked up and spied Ned, but one look at his face was enough to make the man turn away, a slight tremor in his hand the only evidence of his fear of what might be coming. Ned walked outside, confident the clerk wouldn't alert the raiders.

Ned's horse was stabled on the far side of the town, near the blacksmith's shop. He was forced to walk in front of the saloon. Ned kept his spurs off, hoping not to attract attention. It was to no avail.

'Leaving so soon, stranger?' It was Sara, hanging on the batwing doors.

Ned grimaced, and was about to continue when a deeper male voice boomed out.

'Who you talking to, girly?' A big man poked his head out the door. He spied Ned and said, 'Hey, who are you?'

Ned kept walking, but upped his pace.

'Hey, I'm talking to you,' The man moved swiftly for being so big and was on the street, behind Ned. Ned figured he had his gun belt on so he slowed down. He stopped and turned around, keeping the rifle stock facing the man.

'I'm no one, friend.'

'I think you be somebody, otherwise why are you sneaking off in the night?'

The man wore a thick beard, his eyes red from drink, but there was cunning there as well. Ned knew this was a dangerous man. His hand hovered near the butt of his pistol.

'Who you talking to, Ed?' Another man came out of the saloon. Ned recognized him, the barkeep from Deadfall. When he saw Ned the barkeep's eyes went wide. 'It's him, the guy who came into Deadfall, and shot Randal, Eric and Matt.'

The man in the street reached for his gun. Ned brought the Winchester down off his shoulder with lightning speed and opened fire. One shot ripped through the man's right shoulder and he howled in pain. It was too dark for Ned to shoot accurately, so his second shot went wild. But he had bought enough time. He turned and ran as the street filled with more of Roberts's Raiders, their guns blazing.

Ned ducked into a side street. He needed a horse fast. As he ran he spied a row of saddled horses tied to a hitching post in front of a brothel. Ned didn't hesitate. He grabbed for the first horse, but it reared at his touch, kicking out. Ned turned to the next horse, which also shied away. Finally, the third horse let Ned mount her. He kicked at her sides with his spur-less boots and the horse responded, galloping away into the night, Roberts's Raiders close behind him.

CHAPTER 10

Ned rode all night and into the next morning, but he couldn't shake his pursuers. His horse was slowing down, the mare wasn't fast like the Palomino, or like Ole Ross used to be. Before long the raiders would be on top of him. Ned reined in his horse near a copse of trees. There was a small rocky ledge jutting out from the ground. It wasn't much but it would have to do.

He reloaded the Winchester and waited. Soon came the pounding hoofs of twenty-five horsemen. He saw them come into view and opened fire. His bullet skidded in front of the lead horse, its rider reining it in, the other riders stopping behind him. They were about five hundred feet away, just out of range.

'That was a warning shot. I don't want any trouble. Just let me be on my way,' said Ned.

'You can't kill us all,' said the lead rider; Ned figured it was Roberts.

'No, but I'll take a lot of you with me.'

Roberts chortled loudly.

'Ryan here says you hightailed it out of Deadfall. Why'd you run?'

'I told you, he recognized our insignia,' another voice said.

'Be quiet, I want to hear it from him,' said Roberts. There was a long pause. Ned kept quiet. Then, finally Roberts said, 'So you fought in the war?'

'First Colorado Volunteers. I was a scout and sharp-shooter.'

'Colorado, eh, you're a long way from home.'

'So are you. Isn't Texas that a way?' Ned motioned with his gun, then trained it back on the raiders before they could inch closer.

'We kind of like it out here. Not as many Union troops.'

'They won't get in the way of you killing Comanche and Kiowa, you mean?'

'That and other things. What brings you down to the border?'

'A gang raided my ranch, killed my eldest son and stole my wife. I tracked them here,' Ned said.

'So you ride for vengeance?'

Ned shook his head, 'No, I ride for justice.'

'Where's your badge, cowboy?'

Ned had no answer for the former Confederate.

The big man laughed. 'You know nothing about justice. We help the local farmers and ranchers against the Comanche when the Army doesn't. Then they look the other way when we help ourselves to new guns and ammo.'

'Do they know you're Confederate raiders who killed women and children?'

'You'd be surprised, rancher, at how deep some of the Confederate leanings are out here.'

Ned grunted, 'If this conversation is about over, I'd like to get back to finding my wife.'

Ned watched as Roberts shook his head, 'No, rancher,

there is the matter of payment. You killed three of my men near the Meredith homestead.'

'I had to defend myself. They came after me.'

'You took Paul's horse. Give it back,' Roberts's voice was rough.

Ned unhitched the horse, hitting the mare on her flank so she did a little trot toward the raiders. 'Anything else?'

'Your guns and ammo. We'll be having those, oh and your canteen and supplies.'

'You want to leave me here to die?' Ned asked incredulously.

'You know my real name, our real purpose, I can't have you talking to the Army now. Besides you owe blood for killing my men, self-defense or not, you gotta pay.'

'I'm afraid I can't let you have my guns, Roberts,' said Ned, his heart beginning to pound, the blood rising in his face. He knew this was going to be a showdown he couldn't win.

There was a pause, and it looked like Roberts was trying to figure out what to do, when one of the raiders pointed to the south. Ned turned swiftly as he heard the galloping of hoofs. Five riders were heading for him, their guns drawn. Ned shook his head, angry at himself for not finding better cover. His horse was spent though, he had no choice.

'Looks like the boys are back from their scouting trip. Good timing. Your guns, rancher, I ain't losing any more men today.'

The five Roberts raiders were now in shouting distance and hailed their fellows. Ned knew he couldn't fight them all, he only hoped these hard men would let him live. He tossed his Winchester on the ground, and Roberts and his men urged their horses on. They quickly surrounded Ned as he unhooked his gun belt and held it in his hand.

'Drop it,' said Roberts. Ned let the belt slip through his fingers.

'Now kick it over.'

Ned did what he was asked, as guns followed his movements.

'Shoot him,' came a cry from one raider, and several others murmured in agreement.

Roberts made an act of considering the request from his men, rubbing his chin in thoughtful contemplation. Ned started to sweat; this could be the end, he thought. He had failed his Betsy. Still, he would face death with honor. He looked hard into Roberts's eyes. Roberts matched him. This stare-down lasted for several heartbeats, no one speaking. Then finally Roberts shook his head.

'Naw, I wouldn't waste the bullet. We'll make him suffer though. Bind his hands, we'll take him to the salt flats. We'll leave him there. He can die of thirst, nice and slow.'

There was a small whoop from his men, and two of them dismounted. They grabbed Ned roughly while a third man brought some rope. They tied Ned's hands behind his back, and blindfolded him. 'We'll put him on Scott's horse. Here, take his canteen and wait, we'll be back for you.'

Ned heard a man grumble. Then four sets of hands lifted him onto a horse. Ned tried to struggle, but he was helpless without his hands. His boots were forced into the stirrups. One man swatted the horse, and it lurched forward. Someone grabbed the reins, to lead him, and they were off. Ned didn't say a word, didn't want to give these men the satisfaction. They taunted him as they rode, telling him how horrible a death by thirst would be. Ned kept his mind on his children and Betsy. Long they rode; Ned felt the sun beat down on him. It would be tough getting out of this.

Finally, Roberts ordered a halt, 'This here is good enough, cut him loose.' Ned felt a rough push on his back and he toppled from the horse. Air left his lungs as he landed. Coughing, he tried to sit up. He heard a man's heavy breathing over him. One swift kick to the stomach and Ned groaned, lying back down.

'So long, rancher, no one's ever escaped our punishment. You should have stayed clear of us, too late now. Let's go, boys.' Ned heard Roberts and his raiders riding away, back to civilization, back to food and water. Ned listened to them go. When the sounds of their horses had faded away he slowly stood up. He was still alive but had to find a way out of his predicament fast. First thing, he needed his hands free. The bonds were tight, and cut into his flesh, but they hadn't cut off his circulation.

The sun was beating down on him mercilessly now. Ned wondered how many men the raiders had sent to their deaths like this. Ned stopped in his tracks as he pondered something. He knew Roberts had ridden deep into these salt flats with the assumption that Ned would try to get back the way they had come. Instead of following Roberts's Raiders back though, Ned decided to go in another direction. He turned in the opposite direction to the departing horses and started walking.

It seemed like an eternity had passed when Ned stumbled across a rocky outcrop. He fell over a boulder, and instinctively twisted in midair to avoid getting his face smashed in. Rolling over on his back Ned felt for any sharp corner among the rocks he could cut the ropes on his hands with. He finally found one with sharp edges and after several attempts at lining it up began slowly cutting the rope. It took him a while, accidentally cutting his hands a few times before he finally cut through the rope. After he had rubbed his wrists and wriggled his fingers Ned removed the blindfold and looked around for a water source. It had been hours since his last drink; if he could sleep during the day and travel at night, he might be able to conserve his energy and manage his thirst better.

Ned lay down, his head resting on a big rock, with another one casting a shadow over him. He tipped his hat over his eyes and eventually dozed off. He was more tired than he thought. By the time he woke up the sun had already set. It was much cooler now, so Ned dusted himself off and started walking again. He tried hard not to think about water; his throat was dry, making it difficult to swallow. Still, he kept walking.

Ned walked all night and into the next morning. When he felt like he couldn't go on any further, and as the rosy fingers of sunlight began appearing on the horizon, Ned saw something he never thought he'd see again. Grass! He had made it to the end of the salt flats. And where there was grass there would be water. Ned quickened his pace, but he was so tired he stumbled and fell. Ned closed his eyes, wanting to lie there forever. But something willed him to get up: his thoughts of Betsy, or the will to live. Whatever it was, he forced himself up.

He kept walking, stumbling along as the sun rose higher. Ned needed water soon or that sun would mean his death. He wandered on, not caring what direction he went in, when he heard something. The soft lowing of a cow. Ned knew that sound by heart, and it was music to his ears. He headed toward it.

He climbed over a small rise, and then he saw a handful

of cows grazing on thick grass, but more importantly for Ned there was a stream nearby. He hurtled down the other side of the rise and ran straight for the water. It turned out to be little more than a shallow brook, but to Ned it was the Mississippi. He fell face first into the water and drank his fill, the cattle unperturbed by his presence. When he had had enough water, he turned over on his back and drifted off to sleep.

When he woke up the cows were still milling around, only there were more of them. Ned stood up and checked one to see if it was branded. It was, so then he wondered who they belonged to. Then it hit him, there's cattle here on a drive, and where there's a herd of cattle, there will be cowboys. The lack of food and water must have gone to his head. Ned kept close to the cattle, praying he was right that they were part of a drive and not strays.

Soon enough a low rumbling followed, the sound of many hoofs pounding on the ground, and the occasional mooing. Interspersed with those sounds a horse neighed and a man whistled. Ned didn't know what direction they were coming from, so he just yelled as loud as he could. He spooked the cows near him, and some of them turned and ran, causing a mini stampede. He heard the shouts of more men as they tried to contain the whole herd and keep them from bolting. Finally most of the cattle were under control. Ned breathed a big sigh of relief as he watched two cowboys ride over to him. He waved his hat in the air so they knew he was friendly.

'We heard some shouting over here, nearly spooked our cattle. Everything OK, partner?' said the lead cowboy.

'Everything is fine now. I just had a little trouble with some outlaws,' said Ned.

'Where's your horse?'

'Well, that's part of the trouble,' Ned said, an endearing smile on his face.

The cowboys laughed. 'Where you from?'

'Colorado. I own the Flying W ranch up there.'

'No kidding, you're a drover?'

'Yup, do my fair share of punching; it's a small ranch though.'

'What brings you down here?'

Ned was getting tired of this question, but answered it succinctly, 'Trouble.'

'All right, mister. . . .'

'Bracken, Ned Bracken, call me Ned though.'

'All right, Ned, my name's Ralph, this here is Tim, he don't talk much. We've got an extra horse if you're willing to help out with the herding.' He handed Ned his canteen.

Ned took a big drink and said, 'Much obliged, I'll help as much as I can.'

'We came out of west Texas a week ago. Had one fellow run off, scared of the Comanche, so it's been slow going ever since,' said Ralph.

Ned walked beside Ralph as the other man chatted about the cattle drive, and his life in Texas as a cowboy. There were ten cowboys and a cook altogether driving 1,500 head to Denver. Ned picked up the spare horse and helped herd up some wandering steers. Ralph rode alongside him.

'You're pretty handy with that rope, Ned,' said Ralph.

'Thanks, I've had a few years of practice. My own herd is small but I only have two hands, so I get to spend a lot of time ahorse. My boy . . .' Ned paused, his throat constricted as he thought of his son. He didn't want to think about that, not yet. He stopped talking and Ralph didn't respond, letting the silence remain.

When they got back to the main camp Ralph told the other hands how he marveled at Ned's skill with a horse and rope. Even said he wouldn't mind working for a man like Ned. The rancher told him to come on by the Flying W ranch after the drive, and he'd find work.

Dinner couldn't come soon enough and Ned wolfed down his biscuits, bacon, and whatever else they put in front of him. He had two platefuls, and as Ralph gave him an incredulous look, he said, 'Sorry, it's been a while since I last ate.'

'I understand, partner, I understand.'

That night Ned slept fitfully; he was still alive, but Betsy was now likely long gone in Mexico. Ned was in debt now to these cowboys for saving him; he needed to repay their kindness. The rancher also needed a gun, he thought as he finally drifted off to sleep.

CHAPTER 11

'Well, that's a hard nut to crack, I'll tell you what. I don't even know what to say,' said Ralph.

Ned had just told him the story of how he came to be in the middle of the salt flats with no horse and no gun. He held nothing back, including his search for Betsy.

'Well, I need help in rescuing her, and getting vengeance for my boy.'

'Yeah, that might be the size of it. What about the law or the Army?'

'The Army is too busy dealing with the Comanche, and law in the West is darned unreliable at times. These outlaws have passed through so many towns and counties I don't even know which marshal or sheriff to go to. Nope, it's gotta be on me to get her. Especially if they lit out across the border. I ain't going to the Mexican authorities, that's for dang sure. But I can't do it on my own, there's too many of them, and now I've got the Raiders to worry about too. If they find out I'm alive. . . .'

Ned didn't come out and say he wanted Ralph's help. He didn't want to put the young cowboy in a bind. Ralph was obligated to see this herd to its destination. Ned had pride too, Betsy would say stubbornness. He could be as bull-headed as any one of his steers, so asking for help was tough. But he knew when he was licked, too. Getting Betsy safe in his arms was more important than his own stubbornness.

They were riding point ahead of the rest of the group, leading the cows as best they could. Ralph tipped his hat back on his head and scratched his forehead. 'Well, Ned, that is quite the dilemma. Not sure how I can help, can't leave the herd, unless Brad lets me. My older brother, last I heard from him, was in Santa Fe. His name is Richard, we call him Rich, McAllister. That's my last name. If you can find him tell him I sent you. Tell him your story and he'll help you. He fought in the war so he's good with a gun.'

'Thanks, Ralph, I don't know how to repay you,' said Ned.

'Well, you could offer me a job,' said Ralph only half jokingly.

'Consider it done. When you finish with this drive come by the Flying W and I'll give you work.' Ned wheeled his horse around. 'I've wasted too much time already. What about this here mount I'm riding?'

'Keep it, we have an extra horse for emergencies, and your story qualifies. So, I bequeath him to you, Mr Ned Bracken.' Ralph doffed his hat to Ned.

'Mighty generous of you, I won't forget your kindness, Ralph.' He spurred his horse and headed away from the cattle train.

Ralph shouted after him, 'Don't forget about my brother.'

Ned turned around in the saddle, touching his hand to his hat as his borrowed horse carried him away.

Ned wasn't sure he wanted to spend time searching for

Ralph's brother. He had already been to Santa Fe once, and he didn't think backtracking would help him find Betsy. Ned hadn't gone far, still deciding what to do when he heard a loud whoop, followed by a 'he-ya!' Ned spun around in his saddle and saw a lone rider approaching fast. He took the Winchester tied to the saddle and prepared to take aim. But then the horseman yelled his name, 'Ned!' and he realized that it was Ralph.

As soon as Ralph pulled up alongside Ned he started talking. 'I changed my mind and decided to help you find your wife, Ned. Forget my brother, I'm all you need.'

Ned smiled, barely concealing his pleasure. 'What about the cattle drive? Doesn't look too good to a prospective employer if you shirked your commitment.'

Ralph was alongside Ned now, taking a long drink out of his canteen. 'Don't worry, I told Brad, the lead on the drive, your story. I'm a fast talker so he must have been touched by your predicament. At any rate he said go on, Ralph, help that old rancher find his woman. We can handle things here.'

'So, he just let you leave?' Ned asked dubiously.

'Er . . . sure did. They've got plenty of hands for the drive. Plus, I'm only seasonal, and well, I just wanted to help you. . . .' his voice trailed off. Ralph looked at Ned with wide eyes.

Ned sighed, and nodded knowingly, 'All right, Ralph, I guess you'll have to do. Good thing too, as I was a mite hesitant about going back to Santa Fe. But what made you want to help me?'

'Adventure, and the chance to move out of Texas. I heard the mountains of Colorado are filled with gold and silver just waiting to be mined.'

'Well, let's stick to cattle driving for now. Those miners

get awfully hungry, and so do the folks back East. It's a nice honest living, don't be chasing riches where there are none.'

Ralph nodded quietly.

'You good with a gun?' Ned continued.

'I'm fast,' said Ralph.

'Doesn't matter, if you can't aim. How many men have you killed?'

Ralph didn't answer.

'We're going up against stone-cold killers, they won't hesitate to shoot and kill you. Did you fight in the war?'

'I was too young, I was fourteen when General Lee surrendered.'

'Well Ralph, just follow my lead, and do what I say. If we survive this, there will be a job waiting for you at the Flying W. All right?' said Ned.

'Sounds good, Ned,' replied Ralph, nodding his eager head up and down.

'Great. Now the last place I saw the tracks of the Dustin gang was outside the town of Bittercanyon. That's where I got sidetracked.'

'I know that town.'

'Good, I need to get my guns back.'

'You're not going up against those raiders, are you?'

'Not if I can help it, but a man needs his guns. This Winchester your friend left with his horse is not in working condition. The bolt is rusty. I don't think I could have shot you even if I'd tried.'

'So what's the plan?' asked Ralph.

'Guns first, kill any raiders that get in the way, and pick up my horse, leave this old nag to someone else's care. Then pick up the Dustin brothers' trail, kill Jake Dustin and get Betsy. Then go home.'

Ralph let out a breath of air, 'Sounds easy enough.'

'Let's go, kid, time is waning.' With that Ned turned his horse south, and together with his new companion they headed back to the Mexican border, and the town of Bittercanyon.

Jake knew crossing the border would be a bad idea. He had nightmares of Dead Eye Conner waiting in ambush for them. He had more experience in Mexico, and maybe even had a gang of Mexicans just waiting to jump them when they crossed. Convincing his brothers and men was tough but Jake figured it was the right thing to wait. 'We'll get there eventually, fellas, we just need to let Dead Eye think we haven't, or we slipped by him. After a few days we'll cross,' he had said.

'He must be scared of Dead Eye,' one of his men, Will, had said aloud to Jim who stood next to him.

'If you want to see how scared I am, Will, go ahead and draw,' Jake told him, his eyes hard and narrowed. Will must have seen his death if he drew because sweat appeared on his forehead. He stepped back, afraid maybe that Jake would kill him. At least that's what Jake wanted him to believe. He couldn't have any backsliders now. This was still his gang. 'Does anyone else have any complaints? I ain't scared of Dead Eye, I'm just being, what's that fancy word the lawyer back in Missouri taught us . . . prudent, that's it.'

Jake got on his horse and prepared to leave Bittercanyon. 'We have to outsmart Dead Eye and we'll all be alive and rich.'

'What about the Pinkertons you say are tracking us?' Billy asked.

'Pinkertons, heh, nothing to worry about there, Billy

boy. We'll give them a false trail to follow and they'll run around in a circle.' All his men nodded in agreement, even Will, so that settled it. That had been two days ago and Jake was still hesitant to cross the border. Their pursuers, the Pinkertons, appeared not to be fooled by the false trail. Jake left Jim at the border crossing to see if they took the bait and crossed over, but they didn't. When Jim rejoined them, he said an Indian was tracking for the detectives. Now Jake was leading his gang in circles trying to shake the Pinkertons and regretting his decision not to cross when they had the chance.

Gordon shook his head as he watched Thomas get into position. The Pinkerton moved with the grace of an elephant, tripping on roots and branches; he was sure to tip off the Dustin brothers. When the detective finally settled into his place of concealment Gordon readied his Winchester. He was higher up the slope and had a clear view of the valley. His job was to lay down covering fire while the Pinkertons rushed the camp, Thomas's way of keeping him safe.

Gordon didn't care one way or the other, he just wanted this to be over as soon as possible. Great Tree had more skill than he had thought and wasn't fooled by the Dustin brothers' feint into Mexico. He had told Thomas and the other Pinkertons they were still in the US, which made the detectives happy. None of them were anxious to cross into Mexico. Instead they had waited near the town of Bittercanyon where the Kiowa had discovered one of the gang in hiding at the border crossing. It was a simple matter of following him when he left that brought the Pinkertons now finally to the outlaw encampment. The ten detectives, eager to get the gang so they could collect their money and go home, now slowly encircled the camp. It was dark now and only the blaze of the still burning campfire and the pale moonlight lit the camp, situated in a low valley with sheer forested cliffs surrounding it. A perfect place for an ambush.

On Thomas's command they jumped in unison out of their respective hiding places and charged the camp, guns blazing at any sign of movement. There was a returned muzzle flash, and Gordon sighed, sighted the Winchester, aimed, and slowly pulled the trigger. Crack! The lead detective went down, a bullet lodged in his back. Gordon smiled at his handiwork; he hated that Pinkerton. More shots rang out from concealed places, and more Pinkertons went down. Gordon helped pick them off until one by one they were dead. As the smoke cleared, Gordon hefted his rifle over his shoulder and proceeded down to the campground. Jake Dustin met him at the bottom, holding his own Winchester at his side.

'Well, it's about damn time we got these Pinkertons off our trail,' said Jake. 'What took so long?'

'It couldn't be helped,' replied Gordon. 'The railroad hired them, higher-ups. I tried to keep them off your trail as long as I could. I didn't know they'd have a Kiowa scout, otherwise this would never have been necessary.'

'At least it ain't lawmen. They hold grudges. Speaking of that Kiowa, I don't see his body. Billy, do you?'

'No, I ain't seen him, Jake,' said Billy.

'He must have run off, we ain't gonna find him, Jake, and I don't want to spend time looking for him. Nobody will care what a Kiowa says. If he even makes it back to the Pinkertons and they believe his story, we'll be long gone,' said Gordon.

'What about the rancher, your old pal?' asked Jake.

'I haven't seen him, he probably went on into Mexico looking for his woman, lost now. Say, where is Betsy anyway?'

'I forgot to mention we had a run-in with ole Dead Eye Conner, he took her as a hostage. That's another reason we didn't go into Mexico; he might be laying an ambush for us.'

'Well, I'll be dipped, that is one ornery bastard. I wouldn't want to tangle with him. We'll have to find another place to hide out and divvy up the loot. Forget the girl, she ain't worth it, probably dead now anyway. Let Ned find her body and he'll leave us alone. Now, get out of here, find a place to hole up, I've got to clean this mess up and report to Snodgrass that we failed. Dead bodies are a lot messier to explain than sheer incompetence. Let's just hope the law don't breathe too hard down our necks.'

'All right, Gordon, take care of that Indian too, if you can find him. Clean up any loose ends. We'll be near the border with Texas, in that small town, the one with the lovely senoritas, Sage.'

'I know which one you're talking about. Leave my share, don't spend it on whiskey and women. Remember I set this whole thing up for you.'

'Sure, Gordon, we'll leave your share. See you in a couple of days.' With that Jake turned on his heels, to rejoin his men. Gordon slowly turned around and slipped back into the woods, a sly smile on his face, thinking of how he would break this awful news to the railroad.

CHAPTER 12

Ned was mad now, too much time wasted wandering the salt flats, then being rescued by Ralph and the other cowboys, when he could have found Betsy. He wanted to make Roberts and his gang of murderers pay for delaying him. Frustrated, he told himself there was no reason to get distracted by Roberts and his raiders. They already think you're dead, he said to himself, why bother with them? Yet, he kept riding toward Bittercanyon. His guns, he needed his guns, and that Palomino. That's why he was riding, and besides it was the last place he saw the Pinkertons tracking the Dustin gang. Not for revenge, not at all.

Ralph kept Ned company on their way to Bittercanyon, the boy was talkative. That suited Ned fine, he didn't have to say much. The kid told Ned he was from San Antonio originally, too young to fight in the war, and disillusioned after federal troops occupied Texas, he drifted west and hooked up with a ranch there as a drover. Ned mostly nodded in reply as the kid droned on. He thought talking might help Ralph settle his nerves. He didn't mention he had been in any gunfights before, he was too green. Ned hoped he wasn't making a mistake enlisting Ralph's aid. He didn't want to write a letter to his ma explaining his untimely demise at the hands of an outlaw.

Finally, they reached Bittercanyon at dusk. The town was unusually quiet. Ned unholstered the Winchester, preparing for the worst as they rode through the streets. 'I'm going to the livery to get the horse I bought in Santa Fe. Hopefully the owner will take this horse as a trade for the time the Palomino spent in his livery. I'm plum out of money to pay him for room and board.'

When they arrived at the livery, Ned had a hard time finding the owner. Finally, a stable hand, who came in to water the horses, told him the owner had left town, along with several other people. Ned looked around and saw only a few horses in the stalls. He spied his Palomino and told the stable boy he'd give him the horse he had now for his Palomino. The boy shrugged his shoulders and said it made no difference to him. With that Ned completed the transaction and took back his horse. 'Well, old boy, sorry to have left you in a place like this but circumstances being what they were I didn't have much of a choice,' Ned said to his horse as he patted it on the head. 'But we're back together now to finish our journey.' Ned had grown fond of the feisty Palomino.

'What about getting your guns, Ned?' asked Ralph.

Ned gave Ralph's question some thought. After his banishment to the salt flats he was angry, wanting nothing more than to get back at Roberts and his men. Now, however, Ned's courage was abandoning him. Not that he wasn't courageous, just that he was realizing he might bite off more than he could chew. His focus should be on finding Betsy and not on revenge.

'I do need guns,' he said at length. 'This old rusted Winchester won't cut it, but I'm not too keen on seeing Roberts's boys anytime soon.'

Ralph nodded his head slowly, but eyed Ned skeptically. 'You know more about fighting than me, but if I was you, I wouldn't take to being treated that way by Roberts and his gang. You have to get their respect, or at least shoot a few of them for good measure so they know not to do that again.'

Ned took a deep breath and sighed, 'Son, you've got a lot to learn about fighting. I'd love nothing more than to take Jack Roberts before a judge and see him tried for his many crimes. Hell, I watched his boys kill unarmed farmers in the war, women and children no less. But I've got to be practical; there are at least fifty Raiders. I've already tangled with them and came out the worse for it. My focus is to find my wife, and these boys have nothing to do with her as far as I know. I've got revenge on my mind, justice really, but I'm not using it up on these bandits. If they get in my way I'll gun them down, but for now I ain't about to pay them much mind. As for guns, well I'll think of something. Come on, if you're coming, I'm going to find Betsy.'

Ned mounted up and started to head out, Ralph sulking behind him. When they passed the saloon, they heard the first sounds of life in the town. Raucous loud noises came from the tavern and an occasional gunshot could be heard over the din. Ned dug his heels into the Palomino's sides, hurrying him past the saloon. No one came pouring into the street for which Ned was thankful. Once past the noisy saloon, Ned breathed easier, thinking he was in the clear. The border was directly ahead now; Ned figured that was as good a place as any to start his search again. They were near the edge of town when Ned heard something that made his skin crawl; the cocking of a rifle.

'I thought we left you to die in the salt flats, rancher,' a man said as he stepped out of the shadows. In the fading sunlight Ned could just make out the Confederate Army badge on his sleeve. Ned knew who he was without even looking at the insignia.

'Throw down your gun and get off your horse. I'm taking you to Roberts. I figured we should have strung you up, but Roberts loves the salt flats punishment, thinks it's more clean, let the vultures pick the bones dry, he says. Hey, Harold, get the other one.'

'I'm on it, Tim.' Another man coming from the other direction had his rifle aimed at Ralph. Ned had to act fast, he wouldn't get much time once Roberts knew he had survived. He would be strung up this time, or shot. As the man called Tim slowly approached Ned, his Winchester aimed high, Ned moved for his own rifle.

'Easy now, toss it on the ground,' said Tim. Ned made a motion as if to drop the gun, but at the last minute he flicked his wrist and sent the Winchester flying at the outlaw. A split second later he leapt off his horse. The raider, distracted by the thrown rifle, moved out of the way, and was forced to lower his own rifle. By the time he had recovered Ned was on top of him, jerking the rifle out of his surprised hands and landing a haymaker to his face.

Ned kept pummeling the man before he could fight back. Tim called out for his partner, Harold, for help. But just as the raider swung his own Winchester to aim at Ned, Ralph kicked out with his foot, sending the rifle straight up in the air, the shot going wide. Ralph quickly drew his .44 and forced Harold to raise his hands. Ned finished off the other bandit with a one-two combo to the gut and face; he went down in a heap.

Quickly, Ned grabbed his rope from the saddle horn

and hogtied Tim while he was still dazed. He unhooked Tim's gun belt and strapped it on. 'Now let's take care of the other one, strip off his guns. I'll cover you,' he said to Ralph.

'Anyone else out here?' he asked Harold while Ralph took his guns.

'Maybe, maybe not, rancher, but I ain't saying for sure. The problem you've got now is eventually Roberts is going to know you escaped, and he'll hunt you down no matter where you run to.'

'I'll worry about Roberts and the rest of his lowlifes; right now you better give me a good reason not to put a bullet in your gut. Now tie him up, Ralph.' Ralph finished tying Harold's hands behind his back, then turned him around to face Ned.

Ned held Tim's Winchester in his hands, aiming right at Harold. 'One more time, Harold, anyone else from the Raiders out here?'

Harold shook his head, 'No, no one's here, we were told to guard the approach to the border, not to let anyone pass without Roberts's approval. Most of the town fled after Roberts said he was taking over and the sheriff hightailed it. No one else was to leave. Didn't think we'd see you come through, though.'

'All right, you and your buddy can stay here all tied up. I've got some unfinished business to take care of. Come on, Ralph.'

Ned mounted his horse and wheeled around to head back into town. Ralph followed close behind. 'You going to take on Roberts?' he asked excitedly. Ned nodded his head, 'Yup, looks like I'm confronting Roberts once and for all. His boys will tell him I escaped, and as sure as I am a rancher, he'll come after me. I've got to stop this cycle now before he comes for my family.' Ned quickened his pace, his heart racing faster now; he was never one to seek out violence, and he had kept his earlier passions in check, but now he knew what he had to do.

'You still want to help me?' he asked Ralph.

'I sure do!' exclaimed Ralph.

'All right, they're probably in the saloon. I need you to cover me. Get on the roof of the building across the street, I'll stand in the middle of the street and call out Roberts, see if he'll take me on man-to-man. You make sure no one else interferes. I am hoping if I take out Roberts the gang will have the fight taken out of them.'

'If not?' asked Ralph.

'If not, then we've got to shoot our way out of town. All right, here's the saloon, let's get you into position. I'll lead the horses around back. Don't forget my horse when you come running.'

Ralph jumped from his horse to the top of the porch in front of the building Ned pointed out, and from there climbed onto the roof. Ned led the horses around to the back, tying them loosely to a pole.

Ned wiped the sweat from the palms of his hands and steeled himself for the action about to come. He stood now facing the saloon in the middle of the empty street. Gas lamps lit the causeway, making it possible to see. The saloon was still noisy; probably all the Raiders and what remained of the townsfolk were inside. He hoped he wasn't making a mistake, but there was no turning back now. He took a deep breath and called out in his loudest voice, 'Jack Roberts, you yellow-bellied coward, you're lower than a snake. I survived your womanly punishment, and now I'm calling you out. Strap on your guns and meet

104

me man-to-man.' Ned shot one of Tim's .44s into the air to emphasize his words.

Quiet descended on the tavern, quickly followed by the scuffling of feet and scraping of chairs. In moments Roberts's head peered out of the batwing doors. Then he emerged from the tavern followed closely by his men. A murmur went up from them, 'The rancher, he survived.' Roberts raised a hand to quiet them.

'So rancher,' he said at length, 'you survived the salt flats.'

'It was easy,' said Ned as nonchalantly as he could. 'Now I'm back to settle things. You and me in the street, your men don't interfere.'

'Now, rancher, that would be mighty sporting of me, but I've had a bit to drink tonight so you may have an unfair advantage over me. How about in the morning? In the meantime my boys will keep you company.' He made a motion with his hand and several of his men moved forward. Right on cue Ralph fired from his position, dropping one man, a shot to the head, and forcing the others back. 'So you brought some friends, there's no longer only one of you, eh, rancher,' said Roberts.

'That's right, Roberts, and there'll be no tomorrow for you. Right here, right now, the street is lit well enough.' Ned turned around to walk a few paces down the street, his spurs clanking together, but not before he saw the glimmer of fear in Roberts's eyes. When Ned had gone twenty paces he spun around and yelled again, 'I said Jack Roberts is a filthy coward, who don't have the guts to stand against me. Are you going to prove me wrong, Roberts?'

Roberts looked uneasy now; his men eyed him, expecting him to take up the challenge. He realized he had no choice, he had to put this rancher down otherwise his men would lose confidence in him, and everything he had worked for would be lost. 'All right, rancher, I'm going to gun you down, then drag your body up and down the street.' Roberts stepped into the street and counted off about ten paces away from Ned, his back to the rancher. He fondled his Colt.

'Whenever you're ready,' said Ned. As soon as he spoke Roberts spun around, his Colt jumping into his hand, surprising Ned, who on instinct reached for his .44 and fired at the same time Roberts did. Roberts's shot went wide, Ned's didn't. Straight through the gut; Roberts stood for a minute, gasping, blood spurting from his wound, then he toppled over dead. Ned quickly aimed his gun at Roberts's men, and a few reached for their weapons, but Ned and Ralph gunned them down before they could draw.

'Anyone else want to fight?' asked Ned. No one moved. 'Which one of you is Paul?'

'Paul's dead, you shot him.'

'All right, then he won't mind if I take back my guns.' Ned walked over to the body pointed out by the other raiders and recognized his gun belt. He stripped it off the dead man and slung it over his shoulder. He spied his Winchester on the ground and picked it up. Ralph had come around with the horses. Ned mounted up while Ralph kept the other raiders covered. 'Roberts is dead, your group is finished, get to Mexico or go back to Texas. I don't care what you do, but if I ever see any of you varmints again, or if anyone comes after me, I'll leave you like I left Roberts, dead in the street,' Ned said to the assembled outlaws. There were nods of agreement, and Ned, satisfied that the rest of the raiders were too cowed to fight, rode out of town, his friend Ralph following close behind.

CHAPTER 13

Ned felt a wave of relief as he left Bittercanyon. He had acted on instinct, never having been in a one-on-one gunfight before. Only now after his heart had stopped racing did he realize the foolhardiness of his actions. He could have easily been killed. Still, Ned thought, trying to find some positive side, he was alive and Roberts was dead. As long as his men don't try to seek revenge, and he didn't think they would, Ned would be in the clear.

He and Ralph finally crossed the border into Mexico. Ned didn't know where to begin his search; the gang's tracks had ended before Bittercanyon. He pressed on hoping for some clue, his head bent over his horse's neck, searching the ground. Ralph kept quiet, other than to say it was his first time in Mexico. Unsure of himself, his eyes shifted, following Ned, his hands twitching, drawing his pistol every time there was a noise in the brush. A bird cawed and Ralph nearly drew his pistol. Ned had to hold up his hand to steady the young cowboy's nerves. The eerie quiet slightly unnerved Ned too, but he had put the gunfight behind him now, focusing only on the trail ahead.

Eventually, they came to a small brook flowing across

their trail. Ned called a halt to allow the horses to drink. He wandered away while Ralph tended to the horses. Absently sipping on his canteen he watched the clouds roll by. A rustle in the nearby brush startled him, and Ned whipped out his Colt to find an Indian, leading a horse, standing in front of him, his hands raised to show he was unarmed.

'I remember you, you're the Kiowa I saw back in the cave,' Ned said, instantly recognizing the Indian's face.

The Kiowa nodded, 'I was tracking outlaws for the Pinkertons.'

'You didn't tell them about me?'

'You're not an outlaw.'

'So where are they now?' Ned asked excitedly. 'Is the Dustin gang nearby? Where are the Pinkertons?'

The Kiowa shook his head slowly, 'There are no Pinkertons anymore.'

'What do you mean?' Ned asked, perplexed.

'They were killed in an ambush by the ones you seek.'

'Here, in Mexico?'

'No, in the land you call New Mexico. They never came to this land.' The Kiowa continued, 'The place of the ambush was east of the town you call Bittercanyon. The one called Jake said they were going to a town called Sage.'

Ned nodded, 'Thank you for the information, you didn't have to do that. Where are you going?'

'This is not my fight anymore. You will find these men and bring justice to them.' The Kiowa mounted his horse. 'Farewell,' he said, raising his hand, then disappeared again through the brush.

'Hey, I heard you talking to somebody,' Ralph shouted as he ran over to Ned.

'Yeah, someone. He gave me some information on where to find the gang.'

'How do you know he can be trusted?' asked Ralph.

'I don't, but it's the only lead I've got. We gotta go to a town called Sage.'

'Sage? I've been there, it's near the border with Texas.'

'Great, you can lead the way, Ralph,' Ned said, and for the first time in a long time a smile crept to his face. 'We may be getting closer, the Dustin gang doesn't think anyone's after them now. We may just catch them.'

Ralph let out a whoop, 'I'll get the horses.' The pair turned in the direction of the Texas border and wasted little time, stopping only to sleep and rest the horses. Ned was thankful for the Kiowa's information, although he never did catch his name. No matter, the Indian had his own concerns, Ned thought. But the rancher's long odyssey might be finally reaching an end; he only hoped he wasn't too late.

Gordon lost the Kiowa's trail in Mexico. The Indian was too good at covering his own tracks, it was no wonder the Pinkertons hired him. No matter, Gordon thought, he was going in the opposite direction, away from the Pinkertons or any other lawman in the US. Word of their massacre of the detectives wouldn't reach Pinkerton headquarters for a while, enough time to give the Dustins a chance to disappear. Gordon would follow just to make sure the scout didn't double back, then he would meet up with the gang in Sage.

He had thought about reporting to Snodgrass but showing up alive when all the detectives were dead might prompt some uncomfortable questions from headquarters Gordon didn't want to answer. Instead, with the Kiowa hightailing it to Mexico, Gordon had some time. Depending on his cut of the loot he might not need his railroad job anymore and he could disappear as well. Heck, he could take an even bigger share if he wanted to challenge Jake. That boy was plain scared of Dead Eye Conner so maybe he was more of a yellowbelly. Or he could just let Dead Eye deal with the Dustins.

That one was a wild card; Gordon had no answer for him. Hopefully, he was somewhere in Mexico. With any luck he and Ned would stumble on each other and kill each other in a duel over Betsy. That might be too much to hope for. He had lost track of Bracken, didn't even know if he was still alive. Gordon wasn't too worried, another few days and the Dustin gang and he would vanish into the wind.

Gordon rode his horse up a ridge to see if he could see any last signs of the Kiowa. As he sat ahorse, scanning the horizon, he thought it was probably a mistake to have kidnapped Betsy. Ned didn't strike him as the type to seek revenge. Of course, when your oldest boy is killed that can affect a man. Still, Betsy could have talked some sense in him, kept him home.

Gordon was about to leave the ridge when he saw a small cloud of dust billowing up from below. Dismounting, he quickly hid his horse, and crouching down behind a boulder he saw two riders approaching. One looked all too familiar, but riding a different horse. 'Son of a . . .' he said as they came into his view. It was Ned all right, and he had someone riding with him. A two-man posse. They were riding northeast toward Texas, toward Sage. 'You do not give up, do you?' Gordon muttered to himself as they swiftly rode out of view. He was confident that neither man saw him.

Remounting his horse, Gordon set his course for Sage. He couldn't figure how Ned knew where to ride to, or if he even knew where to go. Ned looked like he was riding with a purpose, there was no hesitation. Gordon suspected the Kiowa must have tracked him down and told him about the ambush. He must have overheard our conversation too – should have put a bullet in him when I had the chance, Gordon thought. Well, it's done now. No sense in chasing the Indian when Ned is heading toward the gang. In hindsight leaving Betsy in Colorado was the smart play. Gordon let out a breath as he picked his way down to the trail Ned and his partner had taken.

It took Ned and Ralph two and a half days to reach the outskirts of Sage. The little town was near the Texas-New Mexico-Mexico border, west of El Paso.

'We'll make camp here before we go in, shoot some quail for dinner, and get a good night's rest. We have to be fresh in case we meet them outlaws tomorrow,' said Ned.

'You got it, Ned. After the way you killed that Roberts fella, I can't wait to see what you do to the men that killed your boy and took your wife,' replied Ralph, with a gleam in his eye. Ned gave him a hard look, and Ralph quickly amended, 'That is, I don't mean no offense, may your son rest in peace.'

'Killing's tough work, Ralph, and I'll need your help. There might be seven or eight of these boys, and we ain't letting them go like Roberts's men. They're criminals every one, and they need to pay for what they done.'

'Sure, Ned, I'll be ready. I'll try to bring down some quail for supper.' He must have seen something in Ned's face because Ralph looked pale as he left. Ned didn't want to think about Johnny, not now, but Ralph's words

111

dredged up the memory. His focus had always been, since he left the Flying W, on finding Betsy, then justice against the outlaws. But Ned knew he would have to face the fact that his eldest son, his pride and joy, was dead. Heck, he hadn't even given him a proper Christian burial. His remains burned up in the fire that destroyed the ranch house.

He didn't know how to process those feelings, his loss, his grief, until he had Betsy back with him. Betsy would help him, or more than likely they would help each other through the tough times. Without Betsy, if she were dead . . . No, Ned refused to think of that possibility. He was close now, so very close, and once Betsy was safe everything else would fall into place. His younger children would have their mother back, and Ned and Betsy would have time together to grieve for Johnny.

Ned took a deep breath, cleansing his mind, and began focusing on the task ahead. He knew the gang had at least seven, and possibly more, members. Gordon had said as much. Gordon – Ned wondered if he was dead along with the Pinkertons. He had no love for Gordon Tanner, dating back to the war. In any case he hoped he never saw that fool again, let him and his master Snodgrass jump in the nearest creek and never bother Ned or his family again.

By the time Ned had started a fire Ralph had come back with a covey of quail. Ned hadn't heard any gunshots, so he assumed Ralph had gone deep into the woods to flush out the birds.

'I've got some money in case we're in need of supplies. I figure Roberts's men must have taken some of your money when they left you in the salt flats.'

'Much appreciated, Ralph, we'll see what we need when we ride into town. These boys don't know what I look like, or at least I hope they don't, so we'll have the element of surprise. We'll get some supplies, maybe freshen up a bit, then hunt them down. You do what I say – my lady's life is in the balance, don't do anything stupid.'

'I got it, Ned, I'll cover you and let you take out the big dog, the leader.'

'Well, it's not about me killing Jake Dustin so much as it is about rescuing Betsy. Hopefully, I can do both, but Betsy is the priority, don't forget that.'

Ralph nodded, but said nothing further.

'All right, let's get some sleep, tomorrow might be a big day.' Ned doused the fire and the two of them rolled out their bundles and tried to sleep, not knowing what the morning would bring.

Jake didn't mind his brothers and men getting rip-roaring drunk, but he was worried they would go through all of their ill-gotten wealth. They had been in Sage for two days and the liquor had not stopped flowing. And the women kept coming. Soon all their money would be gone and they would have to take to robbing banks and stages again. Jake didn't want that; this last score with the railway, that Gordon helped set up, was supposed to set him up for life. But they had to be smart with their money, not spend it on women and whiskey. Especially since sooner than he liked they would really be wanted men. When word of the Pinkerton massacre got out the prices on their heads would double or even triple. As soon as Gordon met up with them, they would split the loot and Jake and his brothers would disappear to Mexico.

The rest of the gang can fend for themselves, but Gordon had better hurry, Jake thought. He was keeping Gordon's share separate from the rest, but the way these boys were going through their money, before long one or more might come to Jake asking for a part of that share. Jake warned his brothers not to get too crazy, and they seemed more restrained than the other men. At least Frank was; Billy could get plum crazy at times. The other six men would be through their money in a week, Jake guessed. He hoped by that time he and his brothers would be long gone. He was tired of leading this gang, he doubted the loyalty of some of them; it was time to get some new blood after the heat died down.

'Jake?' Frank had sidled up to him while he was deep in repose. He was sitting in the farthest corner of one of the Sage's three saloons. It was the dankest, dirtiest, and therefore cheapest of the three.

'Yeah, Frank?'

'We've got to do something about Billy, he's getting too carried away with his money. Him and the other guys are over at the Thirsty Spittoon and drinking and gambling so much I don't know how long till his money is gone,' said Frank, a worried look on his face.

'I warned him. But the durned fool can't stay away from trouble when he gets with the other guys and they get to drinking. We've got to separate ourselves from the rest of the gang and take Billy with us to save him from himself.'

Frank nodded, 'What do you want to do, Jake?'

'We're pulling up stakes first thing in the morning, you, me and Billy. We'll take Gordon's share with us in case we run into him. We'll head across the border through El Paso. I don't think Dead Eye will wait for us there. Once the rest of the gang either sobers up or disappears in a few days, we'll come back to Sage. If we don't see Gordon, we'll keep his share,' said Jake.

'Then?' pressed Frank.

'Then, it could be anywhere, Arizona, California, hell even Alaska. Or we can go back to Mexico. I'm hoping this money will last us a long time, and we won't have to rob anymore. With any luck there won't be too much fuss over the Pinkertons' deaths, or at least it's something we can blame the rest of the gang for.'

'Sounds good, Jake. So what do I tell Billy?' asked Frank.

'Don't tell him anything, not now. Pack up his belongings, saddle up his horse in the morning, and when he gets up, tell him . . .' Jake paused, then a sly smile crept across his face, 'tell him we're having a family meeting outside of town.'

'You got it, Jake,' said Frank, then he left to pack the gear. Jake leaned back, satisfied that he could keep his family together with the majority of their loot. The rest of the gang would figure out they left, but Jake doubted they would care. Not while they still had money. When they ran out, then they would care where Jake and his brothers went, but by that time the Dustin brothers would be long gone.

CHAPTER 14

The town of Sage was bigger than Bittercanyon, nearly as big as Colorado City. Ned figured with it being close to El Paso there were a lot of cowboys who came here. It sprung up soon after the war ended when cattle drives started becoming more popular. That made Sage a boom town, here today, gone tomorrow. In the meantime, Ned observed as he and Ralph rode down the main street, it served nicely as a hideout for outlaws.

'We'll stop at the first saloon we see and start asking around,' Ned said as he turned in his saddle to eye Ralph. 'Your guns loaded?'

'Yep, I've got them loaded and ready to go, Ned.'

'Good. I hope we don't need them, but with this group we've got to be prepared.'

'I thought we were going in guns blazing?' asked Ralph, a hint of disappointment in his voice.

'That might still happen, but I figure Dustin and his gang, thinking now that the Pinkertons are gone nobody is on their trail, might be letting off some steam. So they'll have been drinking and carousing all night long. It might be that we can catch them off guard.'

'All right, well I'm just going to follow you, Ned.'

'That's a good lad,' Ned said, smiling to himself.

The first saloon they came across was closed, the sign saying it didn't open until noon. The second saloon was open, so Ned and Ralph hitched their horses to the rail and walked inside.

'What can I get for you this early in the morning?' asked the barkeep.

'Two whiskeys,' said Ned. He was about to ask the bar-keeper if he had seen a group of men come in the past week, but he stopped himself. He wasn't sure how many new friends the Dustin gang had made in Sage, and was concerned he might tip them off that they were being hunted. Instead he thanked the man for the whiskeys. Ralph promptly paid him. Ned turned around and scanned the empty parlor floor, drink in hand. He didn't want to drink it, not yet. Ned knew alcohol would slow his reaction time. The rancher needed to be as fast as possible if it came down to gunslinging against the Dustin brothers and their lackeys.

Ralph had no such compunctions. He quickly downed his whiskey and asked for another one. 'Sorry, nerves,' he responded to an annoyed glance from Ned.

'Just relax, Ralph, ain't nothing happening yet. When it does happen, it will be so quick you won't have time to think about it.'

'Like with Roberts?' asked Ralph.

'Yeah, just like Roberts, and the war . . .' said Ned, trail-ing off as he eyed the stairs. A man stumbled out of a room upstairs, wearing nothing but his long johns, and was making his way toward the bar. The unsteady gait of the man told Ned he was either half asleep or still drunk from the night before. Either way he might be a good source of information. The man was not small; his muscles bulged under his clothes. Ned sized him up as he finally made it to the bar. There was something oddly familiar about him.

'Another whiskey?' asked the barkeep.

'Just give me the whole bottle, Simon, I'm going back upstairs. What are you looking at?' said the man as he noticed Ned eyeing him.

The two engaged in a short stare-down until Ned said, 'Nothing, friend, just thought I knew you from some place.'

'I'm sure I don't know you, now get out of my way.'

'Umm, there is the matter of payment. . . .' said Simon.

'Just put it on my tab, I'm good for it.'

'Well, Larry, I mean Mr Hodgkin, you and your friends have been spending a lot of money, and now you're putting things on credit. And my boss will have my hide if I don't account for things like missing bottles of whiskey. I'm just worried you're running out of money. . . .' Simon trailed off meekly.

Larry puffed himself up to his full height and Ned was afraid he was going to strike the bartender. His hand glided toward his Colt. But then Larry leaned in close to Simon's face and harshly whispered, 'Trust me when I say I'm good for the money. Hell, we're all good for the money, me and my friends, that is.' He gave Ned a dirty look. 'Now put this whiskey bottle on my tab and don't mention money to me again.'

Simon had gone pale, but he quickly wrote down Larry's tab. With that the man stomped back upstairs, swigging whiskey as he went. Ned turned to Simon when the big man was out of earshot, rumbling up the stairs. 'Tell me, did he come into town recently with about seven or eight friends?'

'They came into town four days ago, and there were

nine of them. Three of them seem to be brothers.'

'Did they have a woman with them?'

'I don't know, there were lots of women around them once they started throwing money about. It's hard to say which ones came with them,' replied Simon.

'All right, thanks for the information.' Ned knew the Dustin gang was here, now it was time to get Betsy and bring justice to them.

'Come on, Billy, quit dragging your feet,' Jake muttered under his breath as he watched from the hill overlooking Sage from the southern edge of the town. Frank was leading Billy's horse, but every few minutes Billy would look back from his saddle, pointing toward the town. His brother would shake his head adamantly and force Billy's horse to follow. The process was taking time, too much time. Jake wanted to be away from here, the sooner the better. When his brothers were about two-thirds of the way to his position Jake heard a loud bang, a gunshot, coming from the town.

Jake cursed to himself and rode down to meet Frank and Billy, too impatient to wait any longer. 'Come on, Billy, we've got to go.'

'What was that shot?' Billy asked, his eyes drooping, trying to stifle a yawn.

'Sounded like it came from Sage,' said Frank.

'Damn, trouble. That's why we need to leave, Billy,' said Jake. 'You're going to spend all your money in this cow town and be right back where you started. That's why we're leaving.'

'What about the others?'

'They're the reason you're spending your money. They got their share, they'll be fine, it's time for the Dustin brothers to move on.'

Jake saw Billy's face turn red, his eyes narrow, and his jaw clench. He didn't want to have to fight his younger brother but if he wouldn't listen to reason Jake was prepared to knock him out and tie him over his horse to get him to come. Jake stared back at him, hoping to defuse the anger he knew was building in Billy. Another gunshot rang out from the town and Jake wondered if it was the law, or another group of Pinkertons, finally catching up to his gang.

He was about to speak to Billy, urging him once more to come, but the gunshot finally convinced his youngest brother to follow. Without a word, still glaring at Jake, he dug his heels into his horse and rode up the hill, Frank and Jake close on his heels.

'We'll head to Mexico for a while, then maybe we'll go to California or even Oregon. Don't worry, Billy, we'll find some new amigos for you to drink with. Of course you might want to find a nice. . . .' Jake trailed off when he heard a shout from below. Turning in the saddle, he saw a lone rider coming up the hill waving his hat back and forth.

'It's Sam, I recognize him,' said Billy.

Sam Billington was one of Jake's crew. Dang, more trouble, Jake thought. The whole reason he wanted to leave was coming after him. The eldest Dustin brother slowed his horse waiting for Sam to catch up to them.

'Jake,' Sam shouted as he finally reached the trio. 'Jake, it's the rancher, he found us. He's gone crazy, looking for his wife and for you. Did you know? Is that why you're leaving?' Sam eyed Jake suspiciously.

'Slow down, Sam, you're talking too fast. You say the rancher is here?'

'Yeah, Jake, he's here, and he's got a friend, some

young buck. They got Larry and some of the others.'

Jake nodded his head, 'All right, it's a good thing we're leaving. Sam, you can come with us. I'm breaking up the gang, those other boys will have to fend for themselves. We're headed for Mexico now.'

Sam readily agreed to come with the Dustin brothers, which made Billy happy. The foursome crested the hill and without looking back rode fast down the other side, putting Sage and the vengeful rancher far behind them.

'Where is she?' Ned roared as he threw Larry up against the wall once again. The outlaw's face was bruised and bloodied, Ned's hands raw from pummeling the man. Ned and Ralph had followed the drunken Larry to his room when he left the bar. He was unaware of their presence until he opened his door. He had tried to swing his whiskey bottle at Ned's head but Ned had lowered his shoulder into Larry's chest and drove him through the door. Ralph followed, his .44 drawn in case anyone else was in the room. There was only a woman lying on the bed, who screamed and promptly fled when the fighting began.

Ned had spent the next several minutes working Larry over while shouting at him, where was Betsy. So far the big man hadn't answered, at least not to Ned's satisfaction. Now the bandit was beat and looked about to topple over. He wasn't even putting up a fight anymore. Before he passed out Ned wanted to know where they were keeping Betsy.

'Hold him up, Ralph. I need him to answer my question.' The young cowboy braced Larry against the wall keeping him standing. 'Now, answer me, where is my wife, where is Betsy?'

The big man labored for breath as Ned drew his own .44 and aimed it at his head.

'All right, I'll tell you. We don't have her. A man took her a few days back. She's gone,' said Larry between gasps.

'Where, Mexico?' Ned cocked his gun.

Larry shook his head. 'Somewhere in New Mexico, I ain't sure where. Jake, he was forced to give her up, some debt he owed, so the man took Betsy as his collateral, I swear.'

'Who is he?'

The outlaw gave Ned a blood-filled smile, 'Dead Eye Conner.'

There was silence for a few moments but Ned could hear Ralph's sharp intake of breath. He knew this man, at least by reputation. Ned had heard of him. During the war, rumors abounded about a man who killed with impunity in Kansas. But Dead Eye's gunslinging past would not deter him from finding his Betsy.

'All right,' Ned said at length, 'where is Jake Dustin and his brothers?' Ned pressed the barrel of his gun against Larry's temple to get him to finally talk.

Larry shrugged his shoulders, 'They're around here somewhere. They're here, in this hotel.'

'All right, tie this fool up, we'll deliver him to the sheriff.' Ned turned his back on the beaten man, thinking him finished, while Ralph looked for some rope. But Ned underestimated Larry; the big man wasn't finished. Instead, when Ned turned around he met a punch right in the nose, then a tackle as the outlaw charged into him. Ned, his adrenaline worn off, struggled to push the heavier man away.

Ned saw Ralph lunge for Larry, driving his fists into his back and forcing him off the rancher. Together, the two of them hogtied the big outlaw, the fight finally gone out of him, and left him, hollering, on the bedroom floor.

'Gag him before he wakes the others,' Ned said as he drew his gun. Peering around the door, his gun cocked, Ned waited to see if any other members of the gang were outside. Seeing no one around he stepped into the hallway.

As Ned passed a room adjacent to Larry's the door burst open, and a short stubby man holding a shotgun charged out, firing a shot. Ned jumped back as soon as the door swung out and the shotgun blast went wide. He grabbed the man's arm and tried to wrestle the gun away before he could unload the second barrel. With his strong arm, he jerked the gun free but the short man kicked it out of Ned's reach before he could control it. The shotgun fell to the floor below. Ned whipped out his .44 and fired at the man's leg. He yelped in pain as the leg buckled under him, collapsing on the floor.

Before Ned could question the man, another door opened on the far side and two more men entered the narrow hallway. 'Ralph, let's go!' Ned yelled as the two men quickly drew and started pumping lead. Ned leaped over the railing, landing awkwardly on a table. He fell over onto the floor, rolling to avoid any gunfire from above. Rolling into a crouch and using the overturned table as a shield, Ned drew his gun and fired, scattering the men. Just then Ralph came out of the room, taking out one of the gunmen with his revolver. The second man backed away calling for help as Ralph closed in on him.

Ned saw another member of the gang come out of a far room and try to sneak up behind Ralph. He aimed and fired, getting the man in the arm. Ned thought he saw a sixth man peek his head out from a door but it quickly disappeared. The final man left standing threw his hands up as Ralph bore down on him, pistol whipping him behind the ear.

The rancher stood up, wincing some in pain from his fall. He walked back up the stairs and helped Ralph with the outlaws. One was dead, killed by Ralph, three others lay wounded. Ned and Ralph bound them with ropes.

'With Larry in there that makes five of them. I thought I saw another one in that far room. Ralph, why don't you take a look while I cover these fools,' Ned said.

Ralph returned in a moment, 'The room is empty but the window is open, so he might have escaped.'

'I wonder if he was one of the brothers?' replied Ned.

'Maybe, or possibly just an innocent patron. Don't you reckon we got the whole gang?'

'Almost, except for the three important ones. The Dustin brothers.'

'How do you know we ain't got 'em?' asked Ralph.

Ned reached into his back pocket and pulled out three Wanted posters and handed them to Ralph. 'Take a gander here, see if the pictures match any of these men. I picked the posters up in Colorado City and memorized the faces.'

Ralph took the proffered posters, studying them and the captured men's faces. Ralph walked over to the dead man, pulling the body face-up to look at him. None of the men looked like the pictures from the posters. 'You're right, they ain't here.'

Ned nodded slowly, 'We still got to find them and Betsy, but let's talk to the sheriff about these four. And even get them a doctor, the one with the wounded leg looks like he might bleed out.'

'These men were involved in the raid on your ranch and the murder of your son. Don't you want revenge? You could say they tried to grab your gun and shoot them dead, or just leave them for dead,' Ralph said.

'This ain't about revenge, kid, it's about justice and finding Betsy. She ain't here so we got to move on. Let the law give these bandits their punishment. Besides, they ain't the ones that ordered the raid or the murder of Johnny, it was Jake Dustin. He's the man I got to find, then, well, we'll see about his justice.' Ned turned to walk down the stairs only to find the sheriff had already entered the saloon, followed by the perspiring and shaking barman.

CHAPTER 15

Gordon rode into Sage thinking he had beat Ned and his partner here. He wasn't sure exactly where Jake and his boys would be, but guessed they hung their spurs at the Diamond J saloon. There was high-stakes gambling in the backroom, and Jake had told Gordon his younger brother Billy loved to gamble.

When Gordon approached the front of the saloon he saw a crowd of people milling about. Without dismounting he leaned over his horse to a man standing there and said 'What happened here?'

'Big shoot-out in the Diamond J. One of the sheriff's deputies said it might be the Dustin brothers' gang.'

'Is that right? Any word on what started it?'

'The barman said two strangers came into town, one middle-aged, one young, and they were the ones that started it,' said the man.

'You don't say? Well thank you kindly, good sir. I must be on my way now,' replied Gordon.

'Say, mister, were you planning on staying in the Diamond J?'

'Me? Oh, no, I'm passing through.' Gordon trotted his horse down the road, cursing silently to himself. So Ned had beat him here and had taken out the Dustin gang. It might be time to cut his losses, he thought, and head back to Colorado. But first he would have to sever any connection between himself and Jake Dustin, and anyone who knows about his dealings with the Dustins, even Ned Bracken.

Ned waited patiently while the sheriff examined the trussed-up outlaws. Finally, the stout lawman approached Ned, his finger absently twirling his handlebar mustache. 'You a bounty hunter?' asked the sheriff.

Ned shook his head grimly. 'I'm no bounty hunter. I had a personal grudge against these boys.'

The sheriff gave him a queer look. Ned had wanted to keep his quest a secret, but he knew the members of the Dustin gang, those alive anyway, would tell the sheriff who Ned was, or at least who they thought he was.

'They're wanted men, I'm sure there's a reward for them.'

'Are the Dustin brothers among them?'

The sheriff turned to ask one of his deputies the same question and the man shrugged his shoulders.

'It doesn't appear they are,' replied the sheriff.

'Then keep the reward money, or give it to some widows and orphans.'

'Now, mister . . . what is your name by the way?'

'Bracken, Ned Bracken.'

'Mr Bracken, Sheriff Dingler, this town ain't no place for vigilante justice. There has to be an investigation. Let the law handle it, we'll bring the rest of 'em to justice.'

Ned turned on the sheriff suddenly, his rage finally boiling over. 'Let the law handle it? These fools and their leader burned my ranch to the ground, killed my firstborn son, and kidnapped my wife. Let the law handle it? Where was the law? I've been chasing them for over two weeks now, and you're the first lawman to tell me he'd handle it. How long have these boys been in Sage gambling and whoring? How much did they pay you to look the other way, Dingler?'

Dingler stood with his mouth agape, unable to speak as Ned continued to scowl at him. In disgust Ned walked away. 'If there's nothing else, Sheriff Dingler, I'll be on my way,' he said over his shoulder.

'Nothing more, Mr Bracken, a clear case of self-defense, thank you for your time.'

Ned continued walking on out the door, Ralph on his heels.

'We going to find the Dustin brothers now?' asked Ralph, his voice pitching high.

'Yup, I reckon they ain't in town anymore. They either left before we came or they're leaving now.'

'In what direction?'

'Since the whole town is alerted to their presence, and the lawman, if he can be called that, plans to bring them to justice, I figure they'll head south to Mexico.'

'Back to the border,' said Ralph.

Ned nodded slowly, his eyes set hard as he mounted his horse. 'That's right, and this time we're going to finish it. Let's ride.' He broke into a canter, putting Sage in his trail dust. Ned didn't even look back to see if Ralph was following.

Betsy looked on the assembled men in fear. Riding with Dead Eye was one thing but now he was looking to recruit more men. When they came across them Dead Eye had been fuming; he had missed the Dustin brothers. He had doubled back assuming he would catch them unawares but for some reason Jake and his men had changed direction. Now she and Dead Eye were standing on the outskirts of Sage, with the remnants of what he called Roberts's Raiders standing around them.

'I tell you he shot Roberts dead in the street then rode off,' one raider was saying to Dead Eye.

'This man, he was a rancher you say?'

'Yup, from Colorado.'

Betsy's heart pounded in her chest; Ned, he was here looking for her. She dared not give anything away. If Dead Eye knew it was her husband that killed Roberts she didn't know what he would do to her.

'Well, don't that beat all, this little miss is from Colorado. You two wouldn't be related now, would you?' Dead Eye looked at her with a sly smile. Betsy said nothing, just stared straight ahead. Dead Eye turned back to the renegades and said, 'All right, your leader is dead. If you want to avenge his death or want a share of a whole mess of silver then ride with me.'

There was a pause as some of the men shifted in their stances, unsure of what to do. There were about twenty of them altogether, which was less than half of their original number according to Dead Eye. The others had scattered to the four winds. Finally, one grizzled man with an unkempt beard spoke up. 'How much silver are we talking about?'

Dead Eye smiled and hesitated before answering, 'Over two hundred thousand dollars. So ride, ride with me and share in riches, leave this raiding life behind.' For an outlaw Dead Eye had a way with words, Betsy grudgingly admitted. Half the men stepped forward, convinced by Dead Eye to join him. A raider who hung back shouted out, 'Go on with you, greedy bastards, but we're staying to fight and continue Roberts's war against the savages. We don't need you, anyway.'

Betsy blinked, and missed the draw. The raider clawed at his chest as he collapsed. Dead Eye's smoking gun in his hand.

'No one else? Good, let's ride.' Dead Eye mounted his horse, and wheeled, digging his spurs hard into its flanks. Betsy, still ahorse, was surrounded by Dead Eye's new gang, their guns firing into the air, forcing her down the path taken by the vicious outlaw.

Ned spurred his horse on, pushing its limits. Ralph lagged and seemed further and further behind. Ned didn't have time to stop for his partner. He didn't know if it was Ralph's horse that was slowing him, or his own reluctance. The border was close now; he had just ridden down a steep hill, easily following tracks left by four horses, the three Dustin brothers and the one outlaw who Ned saw flee. Four men. He could take them alone if Ralph wasn't up for the fight. He'd make Jake Dustin tell him where Betsy was with his dying breath.

Before he wore his horse out Ned finally eased up, sawing on the reins, as he crossed over a wide stretch of land. A single sign marked the border. Ned was on guard. He made sure his rifle was easily accessible and his right hand hovered close to his .44. Soon Ralph caught up to him. Ned gave him a sidelong glance. 'Didn't know if you were going to make it,' he said.

'Sorry, my horse is tired.'

The hairs on the back of Ned's neck stood on end; something wasn't right with the boy. It was the first time he had lied to Ned.

'It will be easy to track them, they must have just left Sage. There are four of them, but the two of us should have no trouble with them.'

'If you say so, Ned,' Ralph's reply was so quiet Ned had to strain to hear him.

'Son, is there something wrong?' Ned decided to be blunt.

Ralph didn't answer for a long time. Ned kept his eyes straight ahead, watching for the trail.

Finally Ralph said, 'I never had much experience killing men. I thought it would be easy. Shooting from a distance, in the dark, like at Bittercanyon is one thing, but that fight in the saloon must have taken something out of me. Seeing that man bleed out kind of shook me. I ain't no yellowbelly so I don't know why I'm having these feelings.'

Ned nodded, 'Ralph, killing men isn't anything you ever want to get used to. It just means you're human, that's all. Hell, I'm always scared when I face down men, I just react on instinct and that's kept me alive so far. The one thing that keeps me going is finding Betsy. Once I find her then she'll help me heal. Until then I keep focused on the goal. Find something you can focus on, Ralph, something good and honorable, that will mean the killing is right, and easier to do. Only remember these are bad men and what we do to them is right, and I appreciate all the help you've given me so far.'

Ralph smiled faintly; he said nothing more but Ned could see relief in his eyes. It was clear he didn't want to talk about it anymore and Ned wasn't about to broach the subject again. He hoped that Ralph would see it through to the end, but Ned was prepared for the young cowboy to bolt if the fighting became too much for him.

They rode on a little way more until the tracks diverged, two sets going east, and the other two going west. 'They've split themselves to throw us off.'

'Which one do we follow?' asked Ralph.

'We can't know which way Jake went but at least one of his brothers is separated from him now, so either way we'll catch a Dustin. Just a hunch, but let's go west.'

They didn't have to ride far when they came across a copse of trees on one side of the trail. A rifle cracked, and a shot whizzed past Ned's head. Grabbing his rifle, he jumped and rolled, leaving the horse to find shelter. He came into a crouch and fired off a shot in the direction the bullet came from.

'Guess we found them,' said Ralph as he crouched next to Ned.

'Let's find some cover.' They inched backward, firing a few salvos to keep the outlaws honest, until they could retreat behind some brush.

'It looks like they're on that rise there, not too far up, but they've got elevation on us,' said Ned. 'We'll need to get around them, sneak up behind them.'

'You go on, I'll give you some cover.' Without another word Ralph stood up and fired his Winchester. Ned didn't hesitate. While the cowboy drew their fire, he crawled through the underbrush. Then when he was clear enough from Ralph and, he hoped, out of the outlaws' line of sight, he stood and raced up a short incline that led to the rise where the outlaws were. Drawing his .44, Ned took a few shots as he charged, hoping he could wing one of them. Ned could spy the two of them now; one turned his rifle his way but Ned got his shot off first. He heard a shout, then silence.

When he got to the outlaws' position he saw one dead,

a bullet through his chest. The other one was fleeing on foot. 'Hey Ralph!' he yelled, 'We got them on the run.'

Ralph's response made Ned's stomach churn as he cursed softly. 'Ned, the other two outlaws are here. They've got me surrounded.'

CHAPTER 16

Betsy couldn't believe the speed with which Dead Eye and his new gang rode. Like a whirlwind they flew through the arid wasteland, hunting the treasure the Dustin brothers held. She hoped the fearsome gunslinger and his men would forget about Ned when they found the Dustins. She wished they'd forget about her too but that seemed a remote possibility since she was guarded day and night. None of the men touched her though she could feel their eyes wandering over her body. They were too afraid of Dead Eye to do anything to her. Betsy still didn't know where she fitted into Dead Eye's plans, what he had in mind for her once he acquired the loot. She had an inkling, but she shuddered every time those thoughts crept into her mind.

They rode on, into a town called Sage where they finally rested. 'I know this place,' one of the men assigned to guard her said. 'Good place to gamble, and the women ain't bad either.' They were waiting on the outskirts of the town while Dead Eye took eight men into Sage. One other outlaw stayed with them, but he acted as scout and lookout, riding back and forth in front and behind them. Betsy sat quietly, mounted on her white gelding.

The outrider returned to Betsy and her escort, 'Hey,

Hap, they better not take the loot without us,' he said.

'They won't,' Hap replied.

'How do you know? Do you even trust this Dead Eye fellow?'

Hap looked his compadre straight in the eyes and told him, 'Trust him? No, but I'm aware of his reputation. Even Jack Roberts was wary of him.'

'So that's why you follow him? Afraid he might kill you?' Betsy, surprised by the words coming out of her mouth, flashed a look of defiance at Hap to show she wouldn't back down.

'Eh, lady, we follow him because we want some money. Our old unit is busted up, our leader dead, and all we ever knew how to do was raid. He promises us a cut of silver worth over two hundred thousand dollars. So that's the reason I follow him. The reason I don't put a bullet in your pretty little head is because I fear him.' Betsy fell silent, not willing to challenge Hap further.

'Hap, I see them coming.' A dust cloud confirmed what the scout had said, and within a few minutes Dead Eye and what was left of Roberts's Raiders arrived.

'They were in town, but the brothers Dustin escaped. The rest of the gang is captured or dead, courtesy of a mysterious rancher,' said Dead Eye as he pulled on his reins.

'Is that our rancher?' asked Hap.

Dead Eye shook his head, pointed at Betsy, 'That's her rancher. The same one who killed Roberts. Guess he's on the warpath.'

'You gonna kill him, boss?' one of Dead Eye's men spoke up.

'If he gets in my way, he's as good as dead. Come on, one whore said she saw them ride south. All this happened just yesterday, so we can catch them.'

With whoops and hollers the men rode out behind their fearsome leader. Betsy had a bad feeling in the pit of her stomach. She might be reunited with Ned soon, but unfortunately they might both be dead.

Ned cursed to himself as the thug he pursued disappeared around a cleft in the rock face. The man fired blindly, then shouted, 'He killed Sam.'

'That's all right, Billy, we've got his partner. Now surrender or he dies, rancher.'

Ned ground his teeth together when he heard Jake Dustin's voice. He wanted to kill them all but knew Ralph would die for his efforts. 'All right, Jake, you've got me, I give up. I'm coming down, just don't hurt Ralph.'

'Is that this kid's name? I thought you adopted him as a replacement for your dead son.' Jake Dustin laughed cruelly. He stopped laughing when Ned came into view, his hands slightly raised. The rancher's face twisted in rage; that last comment had hit him in the gut. As he moved around Jake, the other man stepped out from behind Ralph, who was kneeling on the ground, his hands behind his head, and aimed a shotgun at Ned.

'So this is it eh, rancher?' Jake Dustin said as he stood on the other side of Ralph, the cowboy's gun belt slung over his shoulder. 'You came a long way just to die.'

Ned figured these outlaws would never let him live. Both looked ready to gun him down. Taking a breath, he eyed Ralph, who was still looking down at the ground, no help there. 'Tell me one thing before you shoot, Dustin,' Ned said as the third brother's footfalls indicated he was behind the rancher. 'Where's my wife, where's Betsy?'

Jake smiled, 'I guess we can tell you, since you asked

real nice. She's gone, Ned, sold to Dead Eye Conner, the best shot in the West, according to him anyway. I'm sure he's got some nice plans for her, too bad you'll never be able to ask him. Now, if there's nothing else, don't move while I shoot you.'

Jake aimed his gun and Ned tensed, ready to bolt. At that moment Ralph, now forgotten by the two brothers, sprang upwards, grabbing Jake's gun hand, causing the outlaw to fire wide. Ned jumped to his far side, away from the shotgun as Frank blasted a barrel at him.

'Hot damn, Frank, you nearly killed me,' yelled Billy.

'Well, Billy, don't stand right behind the rancher. Duck, he's getting his gun.'

Ned took advantage of the brothers' argument and unholstered his Colt. He shot first at Billy, thinking he was out of the shotgun's range. The younger Dustin brother yelped as a shot came near him and scrambled for cover. The shotgun blasted its second barrel, but came short of hitting the rancher. Ned could see Ralph still struggling with Jake. He fired once more at the shotgun-toting Frank, getting him in the arm, and then turned his gun on Jake, 'Ralph, get clear, give me a shot.'

Ralph stopped grappling with the outlaw and pushed himself away. Jake swung his right arm, cuffing Ralph with the butt of his gun as the cowboy fled. Changing grips, the outlaw aimed and fired at the rancher. The shot barely missed Ned's shoulder. Gritting his teeth, he shot back, forcing the outlaw to find cover. Ned rushed to Ralph's side, the cowboy looking dazed but otherwise OK.

'Can you stand?' Ned asked him.

Ralph nodded as he found his feet.

'Go and find the horses, there's a spare pistol in one of my saddle-bags.'

'They got the jump on me, Ned, I couldn't do nothing about it.'

'It's all right, Ralph, it happens, at least we're both alive. Now come on, they're going to regroup.' Ned hurried Ralph along, firing back at the Dustin brothers as they made their way to the horses. The Palomino hadn't gone too far, but Ralph's horse was nowhere to be seen, spooked by the gunfight, or had just wandered off. Ned took out his spare Colt; it was old, in need of cleaning, but it still worked.

'Stay close to me, I don't want us to be split up.' Ralph winced at Ned's words, and the rancher feared the kid was worried he would be captured again.

'Don't worry, Ralph, we just need to concentrate fire-power. At least that's what the artillery major kept telling us back in the war.'

'They're coming.'

'Get ready,' Ned said, his mouth a thin line on his face. The three outlaws fanned out, approaching cautiously. Frank, in the middle, had abandoned his shotgun for a Winchester. Ned and Ralph fell back behind their remaining mount. Using the horse as a shield the two men ducked for cover as the first barrage of bullets rained down. The Palomino, spooked by the gunfire, reared up as he bolted from the battle.

While his horse distracted the Dustins, Ned dived into a shallow trench. He trained his Colt and fired, scattering the three men.

'Looks like we might be in a standoff,' he muttered to Ralph who lay flat on his belly nearby.

'Why do you say that?'

'Those brothers will find cover just like we did, and we'll try to pick each other off until one of us gets lucky, or the other side gets careless.'

'Sounds like you've been in this situation before,' said Ralph.

'It was like that during the war. What we've gotta do is change the situation.'

'How do we do that?'

'I've got an idea,' Ned replied. 'Just give me some cover.'

Ralph nodded mutely in response. Ned, pulling out his hunting knife, crouched low and signaled to Ralph. Without warning he dashed directly away from the shallow ditch into a strand of brush that lay beyond the road. Ned could hear Ralph's Colt firing. He wished he could have left his Winchester for the young cowboy, but Ned knew he needed it. West of the copse was a short rise that led to the larger hills surrounding the Dustins' ambush site. Ned didn't think he'd get a good shot; darkness had fallen, so he'd be shooting blind. Still, it might be enough to scare the outlaw family into fleeing.

The shooting below died down, and Ned wondered if Ralph had enough bullets, or if they'd shot him. Ned put the Winchester to his shoulder and took aim. The rifle kicked hard as he fired, Ned hoped, in the direction of the Dustin brothers. There was silence, then a faint rustling sound, growing louder. Someone was coming up the ridge. Ned cocked his Winchester, thought better of it and drew his .44. Before he could fire, a familiar voice said 'Wait, Ned, it's me.'

'Dang, Ralph, you scared the bejezus out of me. What happened?'

'I ran out of bullets so I hightailed it. I don't know where the Dustin brothers are, I thought they'd follow me.'

'They're likely being cautious. I've got the high ground, and we've already had a run-in with me having the high ground. Let's watch our backs, they might circle around.'

Ned picked up his Winchester and gave Ralph some extra bullets for his revolver. It was dark now, no way to see the Dustins coming. But just as Ralph had made a noise while scrambling up the scree on the ridge so another faint sound came to Ned's ear.

'Get ready, they're coming.' Ned wiped his hands on his jeans, sweat now coming from his palms. It's one thing to shoot a man in the sunlight, but shooting blind in the dark, there's no telling what could happen.

Ned heard a sound again and fired his rifle. The muzzle blast was bright, too bright. He cursed himself for being a fool as answering bullets zinged at him. Ducking just as a shot whistled over his head, he ate dirt. Ralph's .44 crackled in response.

'I see them, they're behind us.'

A loud bellow erupted from behind Ned, in the direction the shots had come from. 'Now, rancher, I'll watch you die, we end this.'

'Oh we'll end it all right, but it's you who will be pushing up daisies, Jake.' Ned leapt to his feet, 'Ralph, cover me.'

Ned dropped his rifle and fired his Colt once. He could see them now, the three bandit brothers, in front of him, outlined by the muzzle flash. The three men who burned his ranch house, kidnapped his wife and killed his eldest son. The rancher saw red in his vision, rage took over, and he started running. He shouted a blood-curdling war cry an Apache had once taught him. For a split second he saw Jake's eyes widen. Yes, you will know fear and more, thought Ned, I am an avenging angel and you will rue the day you came to my ranch. He aimed his revolver at the nearest brother, standing thirty feet away now, and let loose hot lead.

CHAPTER 17

Jake could barely breathe as he watched Billy fall. The rancher, Ned, had just gut shot him. Frank had already reached Billy's side so Jake turned his grief into anger and aimed his pistol at the homesteader. Too late, the cowboy who had accompanied Ned had come up beside Jake, cocking his Colt and pressing the barrel against the outlaw's ear.

'Drop it, or you'll die just like your brother,' said the cowboy.

Jake turned with daggers in his eyes, about to pummel the young upstart when he heard a weak voice.

'I ain't dead yet, he only winged me.'

'That's right, Jake,' Frank confirmed.

Before Jake could respond, he felt a hard blow in the back of his head, causing him to stagger. 'I said drop your gun.' The cowhand cocked his own gun.

Jake let his iron loose from his fingers, and it hit the ground with a clatter. The rancher walked over to him. He frowned, 'I just wounded your brother, but I meant to kill him. The three of you won't face vigilante justice, although for what you did to me and mine, I think I am well within my rights to have you swing from a tree. But no, I ain't gonna do that, instead I will turn you over to the law. I reckon you've hurt or killed dozens of others, or robbed them of their money. It would be selfish of me to take the law into my own hands as much as I want to. You killed my boy and for that I will see you hang. Ralph, bring the rope, did you disarm the other one?'

'Yup, I took care of him,' said Ralph. Within moments, with the rancher holding a shotgun on him and his brothers, Jake had his hands bound tightly behind his back.

'All right, get their horses and all that silver and money. Whatever is left we'll turn over to the marshal in Sage. Let's get across the border and drop these criminals off and get back on the trail for Betsy.' Without another word the rancher and the cowboy busied themselves with preparing to leave while Jake and his brothers sat in a semicircle, hands bound.

'Can you get loose, Jake?' asked Frank. 'Billy's still having a tough time.'

'I thought they bandaged him up.'

'They did, Jake, but I need to see a doctor, still bleeding a little,' said Billy.

'These knots are too tight and aw nuts, here they come. . .' Jake let his voice trail off as their two captors strolled up to them.

'All right, the horses are ready, let's hoist them onto their backs,' said Ned. One by one Ned and Ralph lifted, carried, then deposited the Dustin brothers on top of their horses, hands still tied behind their backs.

'Ralph will lead the horses, and I'll ride behind you. Any attempt to escape will result in buckshot in your back.' The rancher hoisted a shotgun and a Winchester in each hand. 'This is your only warning.'

'The silver?' Jake asked hopefully.

'That rides with me. Let's move 'em out.' And with a whistle and holding a lead rope Ralph nudged his horse gently down the path, the Dustin brothers' horses tied to the lead rope following, with Ned pulling Sam's horse filled with supplies and saddle-bags of silver bringing up the rear. They rode on in silence, stopping occasionally to give water and food to the outlaws. Jake gathered that Ned Bracken was a fair man and wouldn't let any harm come to him or his brothers, but he also knew the rancher would turn over the Dustins to the town marshal and that meant only one thing, swinging from the end of a rope. He had to convince Ned to cut him, Frank and Billy loose.

He cleared his throat. 'Ned, Mr Bracken sir, may I call you Ned?'

'Suddenly found your manners eh? I only let my friends call me Ned. Scum like you can call me Mr Bracken or rancher.'

'OK mister rancher I just wanted to say something to you. Something you might want to hear.'

'Not interested,' came the flat reply.

'It's about our raid on your homestead. Well, it wasn't a random target. We were told to hit your place, specifically.'

Ned stopped his horse, his attention fully on Jake. 'Told by who?' His breath had quickened and Jake smiled.

'Ah, for that bit of information we'd need to strike a deal.'

'OK, here's the deal, you tell me and I won't blast you or your brothers to kingdom come.'

Jake heard the Winchester cock. 'You won't shoot me, you're too law-abiding. Besides you'll never find out if I'm dead, my brothers won't talk.'

The homesteader paused, considering his words. 'I'd shoot you no problem, but I need you alive. Tell me what

144

you know and I'll talk to the marshal about going easy on you. But I can't let you go.'

'At least let my brothers go.'

'No.' And Jake looked into Ned's eyes and saw no compromise there. The rancher wasn't going to budge, but perhaps, Jake thought, he could gain some leverage.

'All right, I'll tell you what I know. Keep it in mind when you turn us over to the law.' Jake took a breath, 'As I said someone hired us to attack your spread. A man named Gordon Tanner approached me, said he worked for the railroads. Told us there were a few homesteaders whose stakes were right where the railroad company wanted to lay track. They had refused to sell, so Gordon thought to put a scare into them, having a wild bunch of outlaws marauder the ranchers. We were only going to burn your ranch house and stampede your herd. It was also his idea to kidnap your wife. As for your boy, well it wasn't my intention to kill him. We'd ignore the children, but your son drew on me so I had to put him down. That's the story.' As Jake finished, he could see the rancher's face twist from surprise to anger in a matter of seconds.

'Do you believe him, Ned?' Ralph asked as he edged toward the two. Ned nodded his head, 'I believe him, because I know the man he's speaking of. Gordon Tanner and I have a history.'

Jake perked up, hopeful that the rancher would let him go, but before he could say anything a dust cloud appeared on the horizon. Jake couldn't help but look at it, and he could see it was moving fast, toward them. Riders, a posse or someone else looking for them. The rancher and cowboy saw it too, and soon enough the riders came into view, barreling straight for them. Jake's stomach pitted as he recognized the lead rider.

*

Ned listened intently to what the outlaw had to say about the attack on his ranch. When Jake Dustin mentioned Gordon Tanner's name he was at first surprised, but his shock was quickly replaced by anger. He believed Jake's tale, every word. But before he had time to react a cloud of dust billowed up ahead of them and he heard the faint sound of hoofs. 'Ralph, get ready, I don't reckon the sheriff has sent a posse just yet,' Ned said as he pulled his Winchester from its scabbard.

Within moments the hard-charging horses were in sight, and Ned's breath caught in his throat. Twelve riders approached them, eleven men, and one woman. The woman caught Ned's eye instantly; she was wearing the same shirt and dress as those many weeks ago when she was abducted from their ranch. Her hair, now dirty and disheveled, waved free in the wind, her face a mask of determination. Betsy Bracken, his Betsy, was riding toward him. Ned's heart leapt with joy, tempered by the looks on the faces of the men who rode with her. He could tell by her body language she was a captive, and these men had the look of hardness, and avarice.

The riders stopped fifty feet away and a man wearing a black hat, with tied-down Colts protruding from his gun belt, rode forward and halted. He surveyed the scene once and said, 'Well as I live and breathe, if it isn't the very man I was looking for, Jake Dustin, and before we even get to Old Mexico.'

Jake's eyes shifted back and forth, Ned noticed a nervous twitching about the man; this newcomer made him nervous. 'Hello, Dead Eye,' the eldest Dustin brother said at last.

So that's why, thought Ned, Dead Eye Conner, one of the meanest cusses in the West. He had made a name for himself as a tie-down artist in west Texas toward the end of the war. Fast as greased lightning, people would say. Soon after, rumor had it that he had skedaddled to Mexico to fight in their war. Since then every so often after a shooting in Texas, Colorado Territory or New Mexico Territory his name would be mentioned as the shooter. Now he was here in front of Ned, the fastest gun in New Mexico standing between him and his beloved Betsy.

'Looks like you've acquired some new amigos, Jake. Well that's all right because so have I. Let me introduce you to the former members of Roberts's Raiders, now called Dead Eye's Raiders.' Several of the men behind Dead Eye pulled out their pistols and shot into the air, with whoops and hollers. When the commotion died down Dead Eye turned to look at Ned. He sat there in silence, waiting for Ned to say something. Ned matched his stare, not moving, not even daring a glance at Betsy. Finally, Dead Eye apparently tired of the game and said, 'And who would this be?'

'I'm Ned, Ned Bracken.' Ned said in an even voice.

'Ah, the rancher, so this fine filly,' Dead Eye motioned to Betsy, 'belongs to you.' Ned fidgeted slightly in the saddle, making sure his Colt was within easy reach. Dead Eye ignored him and continued talking. 'I've heard a lot about you. You're the one who killed Roberts in a standoff. Some of my boys might be wanting to take a little revenge on you. And of course, this filly is a nice prize. Perhaps I'll let the boys take her for a ride right before your dying eyes.' There was a casualness to his voice that belied his confidence. This was a man who feared nothing.

'But before we get to that, there is the matter of this

silver shipment and the money owed to me by you, Jake Dustin. A good thing for you I caught you in the territory rather than Mexico, it might have been harder to track you. Now where's that silver?'

Ned made his play, 'It's right here, Dead Eye. Let my wife go and we'll talk about an exchange.' Ned held up the reins of the trailing horse, loaded with the bags of silver.

Dead Eye laughed, 'There's nothing to talk about, Ned, I'm taking the silver and I'm taking your wife. Anything unclear about that?'

'We'll see about that, Dead Eye.'

Dead Eye tilted his head and squinted, 'I outgun you – even without my men, I could take the five of you. Just because you outdrew a drunk Roberts doesn't mean you can outdraw me. Roberts was slow, much slower than me.'

'Bold words said in front of Roberts's men. I might take you up on that challenge.'

'Heh, heh, heh,' Dead Eye chuckled. 'You've got stones, rancher, I'll give you that. Now enough games, hand over the silver now.'

'Ned, untie me, my brothers and I will help you fight Dead Eye, and you can get back your wife,' Jake Dustin said into Ned's ear.

Ralph had backed his horse toward Ned's when the riders showed up and overhearing the conversation, nodded his concurrence. 'Ned, there's eleven of them, including Dead Eye. I don't think any one of us can take him. We might stand a chance with five of us.'

'What are you three whispering about? How hard is it to hand over the silver?'

'All right, Dead Eye, you win, I'll give you the silver,' Ned said. Ignoring both Jake and Ralph he took the packhorse by the reins and rode slowly to where Dead Eye and his men were sitting ahorse. He gave a furtive glance toward Betsy. One raider had jumped on the back of her horse and now held a knife to her throat. Next to her was Dead Eye, with the rest of his raiders crowded behind him.

'Nice and easy, rancher, put up those hands. All right, good, now just hand over the reins and we'll be on our way,' said Dead Eye, his eyes gleaming with avarice. Ned kept his hands well away from his gun belt, and when he was within ten feet of the outlaws he stopped his horse, while guiding the packhorse so it was level with his own.

'Far enough, I'll take it from here.' Dead Eye urged his own horse forward. Before the gunman could reach him Ned dropped the packhorse's reins and kicked its flank hard with his boot. The horse bucked and ran off away from them.

'What the. . . .' Dead Eye instinctively turned to follow the horse and in that moment Ned drew his Colt. The bandito who held Betsy at knife point was likewise distracted by the horse running off. Ned wasted no time; before the raider could swivel his head, the rancher edged forward. Betsy, guessing what her husband planned, ducked her head, leaving the outlaw's head completely exposed. He tottered backward, falling to the ground, the knife clattering next to him, a bullet between his eyes.

'Betsy, get out of there!' Ned shouted, and his wife wasted no time urging her mount away from her captors. The shot from Ned and the death of their compadre had aroused the other raiders. Forgotten was the silver-laden horse, still trotting away. 'Kill him!' shouted Dead Eye, 'Kill them all!'

Ned weaved back and forth as the raiders started gunning for him. But suddenly they pulled back; Ned turned around and saw the Dustin brothers, now freed and armed, with Ralph, charging after the raiders. Ned switched to his Winchester and opened fire, downing two more raiders, as they milled about in confusion. With the odds more even, the Dustins and Ralph hit the raiders hard. When the dust settled four more raiders lay dead or dying on the ground. The other three decided to vamoose it, turned tail and didn't look back.

Relief washed over Ned. He saw Betsy over to the side, shaking a bit. He dismounted and ran over to her. Betsy smiled faintly at him, then as he picked her up off her horse, started sobbing. 'Oh Ned, I thought I'd never see you again.'

'There, there, Betsy, I found you, you'll be safe now. I won't let anyone harm you again.' He never wanted to let her go, emotion almost overwhelmed him, but he kept to his stoicism.

'Such sweet sentimentality, but now I'm afraid I'm going to have to end this party. By myself, it seems.' Dead Eye had dismounted from his horse, the Dustin brothers circling around him.

'Walk away. You're outgunned, Dead Eye,' said Jake Dustin as he leveled a Colt at the gunslinger.

Dead Eye smiled once, and Ned's blood froze. Too late he tried to call out. Quick as lightning Dead Eye drew and spun around as he shot all three Dustin brothers, killing them instantly. 'That never stopped me before,' the tie-down artist said as the Dustin brothers fell lifeless to the ground.

'Now, rancher, it's your turn.' Dead Eye was coming straight for him and Betsy, his gun already drawn.

CHAPTER 18

Ned guarded Betsy with his body as Dead Eye approached them. In a few moments he would be within firing range with his Colt. Before he could get there, Ralph, who Ned had forgotten about, still mounted, riding hard, came full barrel at the gunslinger. With a bored expression Dead Eye took one glance, fired and dropped Ralph from his horse.

'No!' shouted Ned. A scream of pain, followed by an 'I'm all right, I took it in the shoulder,' came from Ralph.

'I'll finish him off when I'm done with you,' said Dead Eye, who had re-holstered his gun. Ned stepped away from Betsy, knowing he would have to kill Dead Eye to save his wife. The distance between them was closer now. Ned's eyes narrowed, he didn't think he could outdraw this man. Dead Eye chuckled softly, quiet and confident as he strode forward. 'Draw any time, rancher, and I'll put you out of your misery.'

Ned made for his gun, and as Dead Eye went for his, Ned ate dirt, diving to his right and rolling as he landed. Just as he had hoped, Dead Eye's shot went where he had been standing. As he rolled, he loosed his .44 and came up on his knees firing. The surprised Dead Eye tried to regroup and shoot, but two of Ned's bullets got him, one in the arm, the other in the chest. Dead Eye keeled over and Ned ran up to him. Coughing up blood, the notorious gunman looked up at Ned. 'Fine, fine bit of trickery there, rancher. I had you beat on the draw, but then you weren't there. Just tell everyone I beat you on the draw so they know no one ever outgunned me.' Then he died. Ned was tempted to kick dirt on him, but resisted.

A man must respect the dead even if it is a man like Dead Eye. He took a glance over at the Dustin brothers; none of them were moving. A closer look showed just how precise a gun shark Dead Eye was. All three brothers were shot in the head. Ned's legs shook a little as he thought about how close he came to death. No way he could have outdrawn Dead Eye; luckily he outsmarted him.

Next, Ned went to look at Ralph. The cowboy's shoulder was grazed but otherwise OK. Betsy had finally come up next to him, assured by her husband's actions it was safe. 'Well, this is an awkward time for introductions but here goes. Betsy, this is Ralph, Ralph, Betsy. Ralph has been helping me track you down. He's a fine cowboy and may be looking for a job at the ranch.'

'That sounds dandy, Ned, but he looks like he's bleeding pretty bad.'

'Sure enough, let's get him on his horse and head for Sage.' Ned tracked down the packhorse, while Betsy tried to clean and bandage Ralph's wound. Soon they were back on the trail, headed for Sage, leaving behind the carnage of the gun battle with Dead Eye and his raiders.

When they arrived in Sage, the town sheriff couldn't believe his eyes or ears. The stolen silver had been recovered and the Dustin brothers were soon to be worm food.

As soon as Ned told his tale and handed the reins of the packhorse over to the sheriff, the town formed a posse to find the shoot-out location to recover the bodies of the outlaws.

'Are you telling me as some sort of bonus Dead Eye Conner is dead?' the sheriff asked Ned, scratching his head.

'Yes, that's exactly what I'm saying. It wasn't by design. I didn't go out there to hunt for bounties, I just wanted my wife back.'

'Well, mister, despite your vigilante style of justice, which officially I can't approve of, I'd say you did one heck of a job. Are you sure you don't want a reward? There were bounties on all those fellas.'

Ned shook his head, 'No, I think I'm content with what I have, especially now that I have my Betsy back with me.'

The sheriff just smiled and nodded.

The Brackens and Ralph waited until the posse returned, confirming that indeed the Dustin brothers and Dead Eye were no more. Ralph was stitched up by the local doctor and after a few days' rest when he felt well enough to travel, the trio hit the trail north for Colorado. Ned was in good spirits, but still nagged by what Jake Dustin had told him about Gordon. There would come a reckoning for that man, sooner rather than later if he ever crossed Ned's path again.

The ride north was uneventful, no Raiders on their tail, no Comanche war parties, and no cousins of the Dustins coming to seek revenge. Ned began to relax, his thoughts turning toward his children, and his herd. Soon enough they crossed into Colorado Territory and approached the Flying W. Ned led the party across a dry creek bed, the land now familiar to him, when suddenly a shot filled the air. Ned ducked, but it skipped wide. The crack of a Winchester fired again and Ned, dropping to the ground, smacked the rump of Betsy's horse. 'Get on, get out of here. Ralph, you watch over her now.'

'Is it Gordon?' asked Betsy. Ned gave her a look that confirmed her guess. Another shot scattered them, Ralph leading Betsy away from the shooter, while Ned ducked for cover, leaving his horse to fend for himself. Ned found a grove of trees on the far side of the creek bed. Ralph and Betsy had disappeared further into the woods. The rancher perched himself on a boulder, his back to an aspen. He kept his gun barrel low to avoid any sunlight shining off it. It suddenly became very quiet; the shooter, Gordon, Ned guessed, couldn't see him.

'Come on out, Ned!' Gordon's voice echoed through the dry run. 'We're going to finish this!'

'I know it was you, Jake Dustin told me before Dead Eye killed him!' Ned shouted back. 'You set those dogs on my ranch and my family. Now I'm going to do what I should have done five years ago. I have just one question: why'd you warn me about the Dustin brothers that night near the stables?'

'Heh, to throw you off our trail a bit. If I didn't drop that little hint about the Dustins you'd come right for the railroad. Not everyone at the Denver Rio Grande would agree with our methods, and we didn't want any undue attention. Anyway, you came right to me, which was even better; I could keep tabs on you. I figured you'd find out eventually, and once word reached us that the Dustins were dead, and you were involved, well, I knew the jig was up. You're famous now, Ned, lots of stage travelers from Sage wagging their tongues about you. We didn't have much of a choice, either you'd tell the sheriff, or you'd come after me and mine. So now eliminating you as a witness is a viable option.'

'That's some fancy talking there, Gordon, what'd you do, hire a lawyer already?' But Ned wasn't surprised when he heard the next voice.

'I told you to sell, Mr Bracken. How unfortunate for you we have come to this.'

'Snodgrass, why am I not surprised you are ultimately behind this. So you are the other part of the "we" Gordon was talking about, eh?'

'There is one more I'm afraid, one of your compatriots from the war, a Mister Beasley, I believe. He is quite handy with a rifle.'

Ned's breath caught in his throat and he jumped up instinctively. A shot blew his hat off. Now Ned was running through the trees trying to get some distance between himself and his hunters. Beasley was who made Ned run, he was the best long-distance shooter in the First Colorado Volunteers during the war. He was working for Gordon? It would be only a matter of time before Beasley gunned him down, long before Ned could even get close enough to fire a shot. Ned darted around to keep Beasley off balance, and another shot ricocheted off a tree.

Soon he found Betsy and Ralph, standing next to their horses in a grove. 'Ned, what's wrong?' asked Betsy.

'It's Gordon all right, and Snodgrass, and Beasley's joined up with them.'

'Who's that?' asked Ralph.

'A rifleman I served with, he's a crack shot.'

'So you took down Dead Eye.'

'This is different, Ralph. Dead Eye was an up-close fast-draw gunman, Beasley is a long-distance shooter – I can't get close to him, he'll pick me off.'

'Need help?'

'A distraction would be perfect. Here, take off your hat; he blew mine off my head. There, now from a distance he might not be able to tell which one of us is Ned.'

'Ned,' Betsy gave her husband a pointed glare.

'Right,' said Ned, tossing her the Winchester. 'You were always better with the rifle than I was.'

She grabbed the rifle one-handed, cocked it, and turned her filly to find some high ground. 'Betsy,' Ned called after her.

She turned halfway around and shouted, 'Don't worry about me. Just get that bastard.'

His mind now made up, Ned told Ralph to unhorse and move away 'Keep your distance from me, that way I can sneak up on them. If it gets too hot, just hightail it back to your horse. They're probably on a ridge somewhere, but not too high, Beasley doesn't need much height to see and shoot.'

'OK, Ned, I'll be careful.'

Ralph was about to run westward when Ned said, 'Thanks for helping me. I can't promise you much but a job, and you've done so much more than what I can offer in return.'

'I know, Ned, but you're my friend now, and I'll be damned if some lowlifes like Gordon Tanner and that railway man are going to put you in the ground.' Ned smiled as the young cowboy dashed off. He knew Betsy would lay down some covering fire to keep Beasley honest, and Ralph would do his best to keep the shooter distracted, both buying Ned time. Time to put a bullet in Gordon Tanner.

Ned crept around the creek bed looking for a discreet

156

way to get across when he heard shots firing rapidly, some scuttering in the bushes, and saw a quick flash of a man racing hatless down the run. Ralph, he thought, just as the figure collapsed in another hail of bullets. His gut wrenched, but the railway men's position had been exposed. It was now or never as Ned came charging through the underbrush toward a small rise.

'Did you get him?' It was Gordon's voice.

'I think so, I saw him go down.'

'Better make sure, I want that rancher in the ground, his wife too,' Snodgrass said.

All three were looking in the same direction as Ned came up behind them. Beasley turned as Ned stepped on a branch, his rifle coming up to his shoulder, 'Come to die, Bracken?'

'Wait, Beasley, you know me, we were friends.'

'Ah, but money talks, and Gordon and his boss have promised me a lot of it to take care of you. We fought in the war together but that was ages ago, now this is just business, Ned, sorry.' The gunner stepped clear of some branches, his rifle ready, Ned frozen, when a shot reverberated across the glen. Ned flinched, but when he looked down, he saw no bullet holes. Instead Beasley, a gaping wound in the side of his head, dropped his rifle and collapsed. Betsy, Ned thought, I'm glad I gave her the rifle. Gordon and Snodgrass stared in disbelief at their dead hired gun, but it lasted only a second. Gordon drew and fired wide in his haste. Now it was Ned's turn, he shot down, making Gordon's feet move. The gunman scrambled backward almost into Snodgrass. The railway man screamed in terror and turned to flee. Ned shot Gordon again as he was getting ready to fire, grazing his former compatriot on the shoulder. Gordon dropped to one knee, screaming in pain.

'I'll keep pounding away at you until you drop your gun, Gordon. You're going to face justice now. Something that should have happened a long time ago.'

'Still referring to that incident with the Cheyenne? Those squaws had it coming, their menfolk tried to ambush us.'

'I remember the report you made to the captain. The problem is it wasn't true, your squad went on their own to find that Cheyenne camp. You raped and murdered innocent women and children while the braves were on the warpath.'

'You were always weak, Bracken, didn't do anything then. . . .'

Ned cut him off. 'To my everlasting shame since then that I did nothing. But now I can make amends, not only for what you did to me, but for all the innocents you've hurt.'

Gordon spat at Ned's feet and leveled his pistol, his arm shaking from the shoulder wound. 'Always the soft one, Ned.'

Before Gordon could pull the trigger, Ned drew and fired at Gordon's hand. Gordon dropped his gun, cursed and howled in pain and rage.

'Now, give up.'

'I ain't done yet,' screamed Gordon and now he drew a knife from his belt and charged Ned. The rancher could have dropped Gordon with one shot, but instead chose to grapple with him. Ned, more determined than ever to see Gordon hang for his crimes, holstered his gun. Gordon lunged with his knife, his right arm hanging limp at his side. Ned jumped backward. The outlaw's rage fueled him, his eyes feral, giving him power, but also clouding his judgment. Again and again he tried to hack at Ned, the homesteader keeping just out of reach of the sharpened Bowie. Soon, Gordon's arm grew tired, his swings became lazier. He was losing blood from his wounded hand and shoulder. After one swing, he leaned forward too far and stumbled. Ned pounced. He grabbed Gordon's arm and twisted, forcing the knife loose. Ned elbowed him in the face, crushing his nose. He turned around and hit Gordon once more, and finally the man went down, breathing heavily.

'Now, I think you're done.' Ned stood over him with his Colt just to make sure, but the gunslinger didn't move. Ned waited until he heard the clumping of a horse walking through the underbrush. He raised his gun, fearful that this was another of Gordon's allies. Instead he smiled as he saw Betsy holding the reins in one hand, her rifle pointed at Snodgrass walking in front of her, his arms raised.

'Well, bless my soul, if it ain't my pretty wife your thugs kidnapped and tried to sell off in Mexico,' said Ned.

'That was all his idea,' Snodgrass said, pointing at Gordon. 'I had nothing to do with it.'

'Save it for the judge. You'll need to get your stories straight. Nice shooting, honey, but I'm afraid we lost Ralph. Beasley got him.'

'Don't worry, Ned, he's fine, I talked to him a few minutes ago. Apparently he tripped while running, probably saved his life.'

'That's great, but where is he?'

'He went to the Nordlingers to get help. I gave him directions. Hopefully Harry and Lucas will be there.'

Ned helped Betsy down and the two of them tied up the prisoners, bandaging Gordon's wounds, then waited. Just as the sun was setting Ned saw a small train of horses approaching the rise. He gave a loud shout and was rewarded with an answering call. Soon, Ralph, Pat Nordlinger, and Ned's ranch hands had joined them, all chattering at once. After story-swapping Ned asked, 'How are our young ones?'

'They're doing just fine, but they miss their ma and pa. Lucas and Harry here have been trying their best to rebuild your house. There ain't much there, but it's a start,' said Pat. 'And this new fella says he's going to be hired on. Guess I'm going to have some competition.'

'That's right, the Flying W will be back in business before too long and better than ever. Let's drop these two scumbags in Trinidad, the marshals can handle them, and head for the ranch.'

'We'll take it from here, Ned,' said Lucas, his ranch hand. 'You've been through enough. Harry, Pat, and I will take these two to Trinidad. Take your wife and kids and go home.'

'Why thank you, Lucas, I think I'll take you up on that offer.' Ned swept his wife into his arms. She felt lighter than ever before, he wanted to hold her forever. Before placing her on the saddle, he said with great relief in his voice, 'Come on, Betsy, let's go home.'